THE VALLEY

William Meikle

Dark Regions Press
–2016–

SECOND TRADE PAPERBACK EDITION

TEXT © 2011 BY WILLIAM MEIKLE

EDITOR, STEPHEN JAMES PRICE

PREVIOUSLY PUBLISHED BY JOE MOREY

ISBN: 978-1-62641-203-3

COVER AND INTERIOR DESIGN BY
STEPHEN JAMES PRICE
WWW.BOOKLOOKSDESIGN.COM

DARK REGIONS PRESS, LLC
P.O. BOX 31022
PORTLAND, OR 97203
WWW.DARKREGIONS.COM

For Conan Doyle, Wells, Verne, Rider-Haggard and Harryhausen.

Chapter 1

The Walker Colt was the most powerful black-powder repeating hand-gun ever made. The .44 caliber cylinders held fifty grains of black powder that fired a conical bullet of two hundred and twenty grains. The pistol kicked like a mule and was as effective as a rifle at one hundred yards. Jake Stratford tried not to think about that as he stared down the barrel from less than two feet away.

From this distance it looked like a small cannon. The pistol weighed in at over four pounds, but the hand holding it didn't waver.

"Ah promise you mister," the youth at the other end of the weapon said. "If you've led us all the way up here just to look at a ghost-town, I'll blow your head off."

Jake sat as still as he could, staring into Eric Strang's eyes. He'd noticed the madness dancing there before, but this was the first time it had been directed at him.

"I promised you a share of the gold," Jake said, and was grateful to note that there wasn't even a slight tremor in his voice. "And you'll get it."

I just hope I can make good on that.

Things didn't look hopeful. Three weeks travelling through the tail end of one of the worst winters in memory had finally brought them to the Big Hole Valley. For the past two days the men he'd hired, and Strang in particular, had been getting visibly excited at the prospect of getting paid. Jake himself had been looking forward to a bed – and some better company. But it looked like he might get neither.

They'd been following the bends of the Big Hole Lake for two days now, picking their way along a track that was little more than a slush-filled bog with ruts in it. Ten minutes ago they'd turned a corner that gave them their first view of Ruby Creek.

As ever, the mountains got Jake's attention first. Blue and gray stone, they filled the far end of the valley like tall sentinels. They stretched off into the cloudy distance in a long arc that Jake sometimes imagined was a wall, built by giants long ago, before man walked the earth.

He'd been brought out of his musing when Pat Nolan started to wail inconsolably, nonsense sounds coming from the big man's mouth like the mewling of a babe. The wagon's wheels spun in the mud then took hold as the big man drove the four horses as fast as he could. Jake saw why when he brought his gaze down to the far end of the valley.

Ruby Creek lay in ruins. When Jake and Big Pat left it in the autumn there had been ten huts on the left side of the creek, too ramshackle to call houses, but home to twenty prospectors intent on forcing a living out of the intractable rock.

But no more.

Only two huts still stood, and even from their two miles distance Jake saw the fallen timbers and ruined bases of the other dwellings. Wreckage lay strewn over a wide area, and there was no sign of any movement. Jake's heart had sunk. At this time of day the place should be alive with activity. There wasn't even any sign of smoke. No fires were lit, and in this temperature that was possibly the worst thing about the scene.

Now, as if his day couldn't get any worse, Eric Strang had stuck a gun in his face. And not just any gun. The Walker would take most of Jake's head off from this range.

Jake had seen something coming. The youth had been itching for a fight for days now. Jake had hoped they'd get to Ruby Creek before any outburst, but his timing was out by twenty minutes.

"I'll do it," Strang said. "Don't think I won't."

That's not a mistake I'm about to make.

Jake had seen many men like Strang during his army days, little more than boys, wound up tight with tension they didn't know how to release, then given enough weaponry to pick a fight with anyone that looked the wrong way at them. It was a recipe for disaster whenever it happened. The Army usually beat it out of the worst offenders. Either that or they got dead too quickly to get into any more trouble.

Strang had never had the tension released. He was near ready to blow, and wouldn't care what damage he did when it came. Jake had seen it in the youth's eyes the day he hired him and had almost turned him away.

But beggars can't be choosers. I made this bed. Now I'd better lie in it.

"Are you going to shoot me?" Jake said. "Or talk me to death?"

Strang smiled.

I've seen more sincerity in a two-dollar whore.

"If there's no gold I swear, I'll blow your head off," the youth said.

Jake smiled back.

"You've said that already, and I ain't deaf."

Although I might be soon if he fires that thing.

Strang didn't lower the gun, but the dancing madness receded in his eyes and he smiled.

"Just foolin' boss," he said and put the gun away. "This time."

Jake took his own hand from where it had hung over the butt of his pistol.

"One day son, you and I are going to have a disagreement that might get serious."

"I look forward to it," the youth said, and smiled again. This time he looked like he meant it.

Jake left him smiling and looked back. The last two of the travelling band were almost a hundred yards behind. The Squire and the Greyback deserter were deep in conversation, and probably hadn't even looked up at the town ahead yet.

And best not to alert them before I have to I reckon.

Jake kicked his horse forward to catch up with Pat and the wagon.

The horses pushed through the slushy mud that now caked the wagon almost up to the canvas.

"Slow down Pat," Jake said as he came alongside. "You're pushing them too hard. The Creek ain't going nowhere, and we'll get there soon enough."

The big man was crying, his eyes puffed and red, his mouth wet and slack.

"Something's happened," Pat said. "I knew we should never have left. Look at it Jake. It's gone. The Creek's gone."

It certainly looks that way.

"Maybe it ain't that bad," Jake said. "Maybe there's just been a big storm. We'll get it back as it was in no time."

"Do you think Jake?" Pat said. "Do you think?"

Telling Pat what he was really thinking would have been like kicking a puppy, and Jake hadn't yet sunk that low. But one of their band of travelers had. There was a hollow laugh behind them. Jake had heard that too many times in the last three weeks.

"A storm? An act of god more like," the deep voice said. Jake didn't have to turn to know who was there. The Pastor rode up beside them.

Although if he's a Pastor, then I'm Jesus H Christ.

Despite the cold the Pastor, as usual, wore only his long leather duster over a thick black cassock. Jake knew that under the folds somewhere sat a pair of army-issue Colt revolvers that could be deployed in less than a second. On the day Jake was hiring, the Pastor had killed two men out in the street in front of the saloon, took them down in three seconds flat and never blinked an eye. Jake had known there and then that this man would be travelling to Montana with them.

But I don't have to like him.

For now the man looked almost serene. Long white hair escaped from beneath a wide-rimmed hat, and the sun glinted off a pair of small round spectacles, the reflections momentarily hiding the piercing blue eyes beneath. When he smiled ice cracked in a salt and pepper beard that he kept meticulously trimmed close to his cheeks. He had a black bible in his hand. Indeed, Jake had rarely seen him without it.

He raised the bible and started to intone in a bass voice that sounded perfectly suited to church talk but was strangely incongruous out here in the wide open spaces.

"I will raise my fist against you, to roll you down from the heights. When I am finished, you will be nothing but a heap of rubble. You will be desolate forever. Even your stones will never again be used for building."

"He's big on destroying things is he, this God of yours?" Jake said.

The Pastor smiled grimly.

"He has a message for every occasion, if you will only listen to him."

"I ain't big on churching," Jake replied. "Never saw any percentage in it for me."

But the Pastor was already back with his head in the book. His lips moved as he read the words under his breath and his eyes had taken on a zealous glint that was equally as frightening as the madness that danced in Strang's younger eyes.

"Why would God punish us?" Big Pat wailed. "We ain't done nothing. Have we Jake? We ain't done nothing to nobody."

Jake kept quiet. Images of naked children, bleeding and screaming in the mud came readily to mind. They were never far from the surface,

8

even over a distance of many miles and many years.
I've done plenty big man.
Enough to send us to Hell.
More than enough for us all.

Chapter 2

"...and then I cut off its balls and ate them, fried, with a few onions."

The Squire laughed uproariously at his own story, the waxed ends of his moustache quivering and his belly threatening to burst through the silver buttons of his red serge jacket.

Frank Collins smiled. Not quite as politely as he'd done the first time he heard the story, or the second, but it was a smile nonetheless. He guessed that was why the Squire latched on to him as the one who would be captivated by tales of far off wars, hunting and wenching. The Squire never tired of telling his stories, but it was easy to tire of listening to them. The other men lost patience days before. Even Big Pat, who loved stories more than most anything else, had quietly taken himself off to the relative safety of the wagon.

Slowly, during the course of the journey, the others had taken to riding ahead, putting distance between themselves and the Squire, taking themselves out of earshot. Frank stayed behind with the Englishman. Frank could be relied on to listen. But after three weeks of it he knew more than he would ever want to know about how to bed women of different color, how to kill a tiger, and how to fight the fuzzy-wuzzies.

Still, the stories of old battles kept the memories of his own, more recent ones at bay, for a while at least. And he was able to drift, not really listening, nodding occasionally in the right places, muttering enthusiastically in others as the Squire expounded.

Then the Englishman went and spoiled it.

"Of course, all is fair in love and war," he said in that clipped English accent. "Fighting men like you and I know all about that..."

Fighting men like me.

Frank almost laughed, but the bitterness was too close to the surface. Frank's battles had started on April 6th the year before, and ended on April the 7th. He staggered off the field of Shiloh, the only survivor of a group of twenty volunteers for the Southern Cause, too terrified to lift a weapon, too inured against the blood and screaming to notice the dying as he walked over them.

He had walked away, and kept walking, always heading north and west, hoping to get far enough that he would not remember the hell he had left behind.

So far it wasn't working. When he'd met Jake in that bar in Fort Laramie he'd been wondering how much further he could get. Jake offered him a share of a pot of gold but the money was of little interest to Frank. Solitude was what he was after.

And if this English blowhard ever shuts the hell up, I might just get some.

Besides, he had no intention of earning any of the gold. If he was called to shoot anyone, he knew he'd never be able to do it. He still carried a weapon, but he had not fired one since that night in Shiloh. The very thought of ever pointing one at a man again made him tremble and sweat until only a bucketful of whiskey would help.

He was so preoccupied with his own thoughts that he hadn't noticed that the Squire had, for once, gone quiet.

Frank looked up.

"Looks like our billet might be a bit more rough and ready than we have been led to believe," the Squire said.

The sight of the ruined settlement ahead actually cheered Frank greatly.

If there is no one left, there will be no one to shoot.

The Squire was soon off on another story, involving himself, a Maharajah, a girl and a clandestine meeting that went wrong. For the first time in days, Frank enjoyed the tale.

He even had a smile on his face as they rode into what was left of Ruby Creek.

Chapter 3

Jake was still getting off his horse, but Pat had already jumped down from the wagon and was throwing rubble aside, tossing eight-foot lengths of timber like kindling.

Jake walked over and put a hand on the big man's shoulder.

"They ain't here Pat," he said softly. "There ain't nobody here."

"There ain't no bodies Jake," Pat shouted back. "Why ain't there no bodies?"

I've been wondering that myself.

There might be no bodies, but there was plenty of blood. A swathe of frozen gore lay near Jake's feet and stretched from one of the huts down to the creek. Over at the corral it looked like someone had been throwing buckets of red paint around. Fat bloated flies rose lazily in the air.

Something got at the horses.

His first thought was that it had been bear, but the flattened huts had taken too much damage for bear to have done it. Above them on the hillside a new scar showed where water and rock had flowed; taking the turf away with them to show scoured rock beneath. The creek banks were much wider and steeper than they'd been in the autumn. Suddenly Jake realized what had happened.

They had a flood. A big one, too.

That didn't explain away the blood, or the lack of bodies, but one explanation at a time was enough to be going on with.

For now.

"Where are they Jake?" Pat said. He still had tears running down his cheeks. "Where have all the folks gone? Where have the horses gone?"

Jake had no answer, and seeing the big man so distraught nearly brought tears to his own eyes.

"Ain't no use in getting into a lather until we can see what's what. Get the wagon squared up and the horses seen to Pat," he said. The big man would need something to do to keep him busy, and that was all Jake could think of at the moment. "I'll check the huts."

The damage was as bad as it had looked from a distance, if not worse. Four huts had gone completely, not even the foundation poles remaining. A long muddy scar on the ground was all that was left to show for the month of back breaking work Jake and the others had put in building them just last summer. The other fallen huts were in various states of disrepair. One had a single wall still standing; but it looked like a good gust of wind would finish it off quickly. Pieces of bedding and linen lay partially frozen on the slushy mud. Everywhere Jake looked he saw reminders of what the place had been; a duster coat here, a pair of eye-glasses there, and a coffee pot with a broken spout that he remembered drinking whiskey out of on a stormy night last autumn.

The remaining huts had some signs of damage. White scars showed in the log walls where something had torn gouges in strips from the timber, something that had been trying to get inside. Jake started to think about bear again. He un-holstered his pistol and opened the first door, warily.

The small cabin was empty. More than that, it felt cold and musty, as if it had been that way for a while. He felt the stove. It was stone cold, almost icy. Over in the far corner the beds were still rumpled as if someone had just recently got up, and there was a pair of boots lying under one cot that looked like they could belong to George.

What's happened to you big brother?

There was no sign of any recent activity, but there were two sheaves of paper on the table, stuck into the wood with a knife. Jake's heart fell as he recognized the blade. It had belonged to their father, and had been passed down to George on his death. In all the time since the old man died it had never left the belt at George's side. For it to be here, now, showed Jake, more than any ruination of the town, that something terrible had happened.

He tugged the knife from the table and flattened out the papers. They were the blank end pages from a book, probably Irish Jim's large bible.

The pages were filled with George's neat, almost dainty, writing which was one of the constants of Jake's life, all the way up from Miss Courtney's Junior School to the letter that George had written that got Jake out of the penitentiary a year early. His heart sank as he read.

13

"Jake. I scarcely know where to begin; things have gone to hell so fast.

"It started yesterday. Sad Sam was setting the powder up in the mine, and there was an accident I guess. The first we knew was when there was a muffled whump. Ten seconds later a chunk of the hill came down on top of us, then a flood of water and rock. Next thing I knows I'm up to my balls in freezing water and there's screaming going on all around me. Just as well we learned to swim in Johnson's Creek all them years ago or I'd be a goner and not here to write this. We lost most of the huts. Them is washed away to God knows where. Three horses, Dan Culhoun, and Sad Sam went with the huts I guess. Leastwise, we've looked everywhere and they ain't nowhere to be found.

"I was near to packing up and following you out Jake. I even got as far as putting the saddlebags on old Bess, but Bill Jackson put an end to that. He was rooting around looking for anything that might have come out of the shaft with the flood. He found a nugget, big as a cold whore's nipple, at the foot of the rockslide, and another even bigger one up at the mouth of the cave, just lying there as if it had been put down for someone to find. It fair put the gold fever into those that were left. Up that hill they went, a-hollering and a-whooping. There were more nuggets lying on the floor of the mine. Jock Simpson got hisself dead arguing with Farting Bill over one big 'un. After that there was no stopping them.

"They all went up into the cave in the late afternoon yesterday, leaving just Irish Jim and me here. Ain't one of them has come back. Jim said he heard gunshots just after dawn, but I ain't so sure I can believe him as he's been at the hooch. He says there's a kelpie in the creek, and he's been seeing leprechauns.

"I plan to leave Jim with the horses and head up to have a look-see in the cave. If there is a mother-lode in there, we need to get a Stratford name on the stake. I'll leave a trail as I go like we did at Granddaddy's place.

"I've put what we found so far in the place where Mother will never find it. If I don't return, it's all yours little brother. Give what you can to Maureen to keep the farm going, and make sure she don't pine away as an old spinster. As for the rest, don't spend it all on booze and whores, or if you do, make sure they're good ones.

"Your big brother, George."

~*~

14

Jake had tears in his eyes as he put the papers down.

Shit George, you can't go and die on me. We ain't even said good-bye.

He wiped the tears away and had just started in on reading the note again when Pat came to the door.

"There ain't nothing but black powder and digging tools in the other hut," the big man said. "And there ain't no sign of any folks. Where are they all at Jake? Where'd they go?"

Jake was about to pass the note over when he remembered that Pat had never taken to schooling. He could write his name if he needed to, but even that was a struggle for him.

Jake held the note up.

"George left us a message. They went up into the caves Pat," he said. "They went to look for the mother-lode. That's why they ain't here. They found the gold."

Pat's eyes lit up.

"Then that's where we'll go, too," he said. "I can't wait to see Jim and tell him our stories."

Jake had been thinking about Irish Jim, and the red stains on the grass in the corral.

I plan to leave Jim with the horses.

Jake was very afraid that Jim, and the horses, were now in the same place.

Chapter 4

The sky had darkened by the time they stowed the provisions and got the horses settled. The animals refused to settle anywhere near the old corral, and ended up being tethered to a post near the wagon. Even then they were skittish and nervous.

"They's spooked, right enough," Big Pat said. "But ain't nuthin' special. Horses is stupid beasts, afeared of new places. They'll settle down."

The Squire and the Pastor went in search of some coffee. Frank helped Big Pat stockpile everything they brought with them, packing it all tight into the second hut. Frank noted wryly that most of the Squire and the Pastor's gear consisted of ammo, whereas the rest of them had brought mainly food and bedding.

Fighting men like you and me...

The words kept coming back to his mind, as if they were mocking him. He lit a pipe and sucked smoke as he tried to blank them out. Big Pat stood beside him, staring out at the rubble.

"We was just getting it nice," Pat said softly. "I had a home. First real one I ever had."

Frank had no words to comfort the man.

Hell, I haven't even got enough to comfort myself.

The two of them stood for a while watching the sun go down behind the mountains. The smell of brewing coffee wafted across from the main hut, but it wasn't enough to tempt Frank inside.

Behind them an argument had started up in the main hut. Voices were raised in anger, mainly young Strang's high-pitched nasal whine.

"You promised, you fucker. And if you don't give me my gold, I'll blow your fucking head off."

That boy sure has a mouth on him. Going to get himself killed some day.

Frank wanted no part of it. He stayed outside, until the sun disappeared behind the mountains. A chill set in that finally forced him and the big man to head for the relative warmth indoors.

Just as they turned away there was a loud splash in the creek below. They both stopped and turned towards it. The sound wasn't repeated, and the shadows were already too dark down there to see anything.

"Fish?" Frank said.

"Ain't seen no fish in all the time we was here," Pat replied. "Frogs maybe?"

Biggest frog in the world never made a splash like that.

But, like Jake before him, Frank realized just how fragile the big man was emotionally. Pat was crying again. He had hardly stopped since their arrival. Frank still had no idea how to console him, nor even how to start.

Awkwardly, he patted Pat's arm.

"Let's get some coffee inside us big man," Frank said. "And tomorrow, we'll look for your friends."

Pat almost smiled.

"You'll help us?"

Frank nodded.

"That's what I'm here for. That's why Jake hired us."

Pat shook his head.

"Nope. You ain't here to help us folks. You're here for the gold. Just like the rest of them."

"No, I'm not," Frank started, but Pat had already walked away. He wanted to call after the man, to tell him that the gold made no nevermind to him. But to do that would be to acknowledge the turmoil inside him, and he wasn't ready to bare that pain to anyone.

Maybe not even to myself.

Frank followed Pat into the hut. Almost immediately he wished he'd stayed outside and had another smoke. An argument raged among the four men there, and it looked like one that might quickly descend into gunplay.

Eric Strang waved two pieces of paper in Jake Stratford's face.

"I've put what we found so far in the place where Mother will never find it," Strang shouted, his voice high and whining. "That's what it says. He's talking about the gold, isn't he?"

To Frank he sounded just like a spoilt child complaining that he hadn't been given an egg for breakfast.

He needs a slapping down. And if he's not careful, he's going to get one.

Jake said nothing, but Frank saw that his gun hand never strayed far from his holster, and he never took his eyes from Strang's face. The Pastor and the Squire looked on. They too looked ready to draw at any moment.

But on whose side?

"You had better tell us where the loot is lad," the Squire said to Jake. "It is what we were promised after all."

"You were promised payment for protecting the settlement," Jake said, never taking his eyes off Strang. "And we are a mite late for that, don't you think?"

"And yet, you brought us here," the Pastor said. "You owe us for the time spent on the journey. And remember what the book says – God loveth a cheerful giver."

"Didn't he also say it is hard for a rich man to enter the kingdom of heaven?"

The Pastor laughed.

"Don't go trying to quote scripture at me boy. We'll be here all night."

Jake laughed. He was still staring at Strang.

"I ain't going nowhere."

Strang had been getting steadily angrier while the others spoke. He pulled out the Walker and shoved it in Jake's face once more.

Frank flinched, but Jake didn't move.

"You tried that earlier lad," Jake said. "It didn't work then, and it sure ain't gonna work now."

The Squire laughed.

"Put your cannon away boy," he said. "If you blow his head off, we will never get paid."

Strang kept the gun pointed straight at Jake.

Frank knew the look on the youth's face, the need for action, the need to prove that you were somebody. He'd had the same urge himself less than a year ago. It had taken the slaughter at Shiloh to burn it out of him. He wasn't ready to see any more death here. He stepped forward, taking out his own pistol. In one smooth movement he reversed it and clubbed Strang on the back of the head.

The youth collapsed in a heap at Frank's feet. The Walker clattered to the floor alongside him, and went off with a bang that rang in Frank's ears for seconds afterwards. The shot dug a two-inch gouge out of the cabin wall.

The men stood around looking down at Strang.

"Thanks, much appreciated," Jake said.

Frank nodded.

"Just didn't want to see anyone get killed that didn't need to."

"Is he deaded?" Pat asked.

"Let us hope so," the Squire said.

Jake bent and checked.

"Nope. He'll have a sore head in the morning, but he'll be fine."

Frank remembered to breathe. Just hitting Strang had made him shake. The idea that he might have killed the lad brought gorge to his throat and he was running a cold sweat. When he tried to put the gun back in its holster his hand trembled. Everyone else was still looking at Strang so he was able to use two hands to put the pistol away.

He had just started to calm down when the horses went into a mad frenzy outside, snorting and squealing.

"Bear!" Jake shouted, and left at a run.

The others followed, but Frank could only stand there, struck immobile by fear, with the sound of screaming in his ears and a wounded body at his feet.

Chapter 5

Jake was first to reach the horses. In the dim light he couldn't make much sense of what he was seeing. He had his pistol in his hand, but no clear sight of anything to shoot at. The horses were terrified, kicking and stomping, but there was no larger shadow among them that would signify a bear or a cougar.

What in deuce has gotten into them?

Jake lowered his gaze closer to the ground. A low dark shadow had one of the horses by the lower leg. It tried to drag the horse towards the creek. The horse squealed and kicked but was held firm by a large gray claw.

Jake could scarcely believe what he saw. The nearest thing he had ever seen to the beast at the end of the claw was a plated armadillo that they'd caught and eaten in the Arizona desert. But although this beast was similarly armored, it was built more like a wood-louse at the front end, low to the ground, with a conical snout, and near eight feet long in the body alone. It had three legs on its right hand side, and Jake guessed there would be a symmetrical set on the other side. Another of the large gray claws rose in the air. It clacked with a loud crack, and the horses stomped and snorted with increased frenzy.

The back end of the thing was all tail, a tall black whippy muscle that rose in a high arc above the beast. It swayed, almost hypnotically, back and forth, as if searching for a target. Before Jake could shoot, the tail whipped around, too fast for the eye to follow. It stuck a long barbed tip in the horse's shoulder, the noise as it went in like a butcher cutting ribs from a side of pork.

Two seconds later the horse fell as if pole-axed, eyes rolling in its sockets and tongue lolling from its mouth. Its forelegs waved feebly in the air as it tried to stand. The low beast started to drag it away. The creature left a deep gouge across the grass as it dragged the horse away.

The horse snickered pitifully.

"Shoot it," Pat shouted. "Shoot it Jake."

That finally got Jake moving. He fired straight at the beast where he judged the brain might be. His shot gouged a hole in the shell that bubbled and spat yellow fluid, but the creature didn't slow. It dragged the horse closer to the creek.

A shot boomed close to Jake's ear. The Pastor stood next to him, putting a round into the creature, raising another hole but yet again failing to slow it down. The Squire joined in, pumping four quick rifle shots into it. The front end was by now starting to look like a pulpy mess. An acrid smell hung in the air, a mixture of burnt powder and a foul noxious tang that tickled at Jake's tonsils and threatened to make him hurl.

Still the creature kept dragging the horse away. The men followed. The tail whipped backwards and forwards, looking for something to strike at. The Pastor pumped two more shots into it and more of the yellow fluid splashed.

We're not doing enough damage.

Jake didn't know what he was going to do next. Big Pat wasn't encumbered by any such thoughts. He ran past them and grabbed the swinging tail, just avoiding being hit by the barb. He got both hands round the muscle and started to pull. The beast scuttled sideways, half-dragging Pat with it. The big man dug in his heels and pulled, but the beast, with the weight of the horse attached, was too heavy for him to move.

But at least it was momentarily distracted. Jake stepped forward and shot at the point where the claw joined the body. Bits of shell cracked and split but it still held tight to the horse's leg. It tightened its grip and blood poured from the leg, dark in the dim light. Jake kept firing. It took three rounds, but finally the claw came away from the body and fell to the grass. The horse was free.

Now that the weight was lessened, Pat could swing the beast round his head. More of the yellow fluid, stinking and acrid, splashed everywhere. Pat screamed at the top of his voice, and, at the top of an arc, let the thing go. It flew away towards the creek, acrid gore flying behind it. It landed somewhere in the dark with a loud splash.

Jake waited for long seconds, half expecting it to come scurrying back up the creek bed. But the night had fallen silent. After a while even the horses went quiet.

"What in God's name was that?" Jake asked.

He should have known the Pastor would have an answer.

"Thou hast sore broken us in the place of dragons and covered us with the shadow of death," the tall man said.

The Squire spat on the ground.

"That was no dragon."

"How do you know that?" Pat said.

"Because I killed one once, in Egypt," the Englishman said. "A man-eater. It was nearly thirty feet long. It had teeth like knifes and…"

Jake tuned him out and checked on the horse.

Its leg was broken in two places, but it did not seem to be in pain; its eyes were rolled up in their sockets. At some point it had bitten through its own tongue. Blood mixed with drool and foamy spittle. It smelled nearly as bad as it looked. Its breath came hot and heavy, steaming in the night chill.

"Ain't no way she's getting up lad," the Pastor said. "I reckon you know what needs to be done?" He bent over the wound caused by the tail barb. "Poison I reckon," he said. "And a fast one at that. Ain't seen nothing like it since my old mare got hersel' bit by a rattler."

Jake had been thinking the same thing.

Sorry old girl.

He patted the horse's head, then put a bullet between its eyes. Somewhere in the dark Big Pat started to cry again. The others started to move away, but Jake called them back.

"Help me move this," Jake said. "We can't leave it here. It'll attract bear, coyote, hell, maybe even more of them things."

It took all four of them, but eventually they manhandled the dead horse across to the lip of the bank and tumbled it down into the creek. It fell away into the darkness. There was one loud splash then it too was gone.

Big Pat had his eyes firmly closed. Tears streamed down his cheeks.

"What was that thing Jake. I ain't never seen nothing like it."

"I don't think anyone has ever seen anything like it," Jake said softly.

"It was an abomination," the Pastor said. "A sin against God."

The Squire was more prosaic.

"Some kind of large scorpion if I'm not mistaken," he said. "Or maybe a crab of some sort?"

"Ain't no scorpion ever grew that big."

Jake picked up the chitinous claw and studied it closely. It didn't tell him anything he didn't know already.

It's big, strong and ugly, and can break a horse's leg as easy as if it was a matchstick.

He stood, suddenly feeling tired.

It's going to be a long night.

"Pat. You stay here and watch for a while, Okay? Holler if that thing comes back."

The big man was looking down at where they'd thrown the dead horse over the lip.

"Do you think those things got our folks Jake," he whispered. "Do you think?"

Thinking was something Jake wasn't planning on doing a lot of.

Chapter 6

Frank Collins heard the shooting, but couldn't bring himself to move.

They can handle it.

Frank couldn't take his eyes from the boy at his feet. And boy he was. Eric Strang was hardly more than seventeen years old. Unconscious and pale, he looked even younger than that. Frank had left a lot of boys looking near the same on the field of Shiloh.

Frank started to shake uncontrollably. Deep sobs wracked his body.

Not again. Never again.

He forced it away, angry with himself for the weakness.

Shooting was still going on outside, but Frank wouldn't move, couldn't move. He was still in the same place when Jake came back to the hut minutes later.

Jake didn't speak, merely strode to his saddlebag and took out a bottle of whisky. He drank from the neck, swallowing a cupful before stopping.

Frank couldn't take his eyes off Jake. Something had badly frightened him and if a man like that was feeling terror, then Frank needed to know what caused it.

He didn't have to ask.

"Something got at the horses," Jake said. "Some kind of killer-crab if we can believe the Squire. Killed one of them. Would've ate it all up too if we hadn't killed it."

"There's no crabs in Montana, Jake," Frank said. "Killer or otherwise."

"I beg to differ," the Squire said as he came in. He threw something heavy to the floor at Frank's feet.

A huge serrated claw lay there, spattered with blood.

Sure looks like a crab claw to me.

Frank didn't know what to say. Nothing in his experience had prepared him for this. It was like something from one of the old slave sto-

24

ries that they told in the cotton fields, stories of haunts in the swamps and zombie that walked after they were dead and buried.

"Broke the horse's leg, poisoned it with a bloody stinger and dragged it off," Jake said. Frank saw that he wasn't talking to anyone in particular – just staring into space, reliving a moment of horror. "Ain't never seen nothing like it."

I know that look only too well.

"So what now?" the Pastor asked from the doorway. "Now that we are beset by the spawn of Beelzebub?"

The Squire spat and took the bottle from Jake, downing a generous slug.

"It might be time to beat a strategic retreat lad?" he said when he'd finished.

Jake was quiet for a long time.

"I ain't one for retreating. I aim to look for my folk in the morning. And if you want paying, you'll come with me."

The Squire looked down at Strang.

"I'm beginning to think that the boy may have had a point about the gold," he said. He smiled, but his hand was near his saber.

Jake spat on the floor at his feet.

"I don't give a tinker's cuss what you think. I'm going up into the cave in the morning. Come, or stay, it's no matter to me. But the only way you get paid is to help me out."

Frank saw that Jake's hand had moved towards his holster. The Squire didn't look in any hurry to back down.

Another standoff. How many do we need before we trust each other?

Frank stepped forward.

"Anything you need Jake," Frank said. "I'm game."

The Pastor laughed, but there was little humor in it.

"I came this far with you Jake. I guess I can go a mite further. But what about this one?" He kicked Strang's shoulder. The youth grunted, but didn't wake. "I doubt we want him along on any expedition?"

Jake looked down at the body.

"I had a mind to leave him with Pat and the horses."

The Squire grunted.

"The big man doesn't have the sense to look after himself, let alone keep the hothead out of trouble."

Jake nodded.

"But we ain't taking Strang with us. He's as liable to shoot one of us as anything else."

"That ain't no problem." The Pastor pulled out a pistol and pointed it at Strang. "Ain't no problem at all."

Jake's going to let him do it.

Before he could talk himself out of it, Frank stepped between the weapon and the prone body.

"I'll stay and watch Strang," he said. "I'll take care of the big man as well."

Jake looked at him closely.

"I believe you will at that," he finally said.

The night passed slowly. At first they were all on edge, waiting for an attack. But none came. Strang woke up and started to shout abuse at them, but that was fixed by tying him to a chair and tying a gag round his mouth.

Jake took first watch, but Frank couldn't sleep. He beat Big Pat ten times in a row at cribbage before sleep caught up with the Irishman. Pat lay down next to where the Squire and the Pastor slept on the floor on thin mattresses. The Squire snored like a rutting hog, and the Pastor talked to himself in an almost audible murmur. The noise soon drove Frank out into the night.

He found Jake on the porch, staring over to where the horses were tethered.

"Get some sleep," Frank said. "I'll take the next few hours and get the Squire up next."

Jake didn't reply at first.

"This was to be a new start for me," he said softly. "Somewhere to forget."

He turned to Frank.

"You understand that all too well, don't you?"

Frank nodded, but was afraid to speak, for then he might have to admit his fears, and if he started down that road, he might never stop talking. Luckily Jake had other things on his mind.

"I'm trusting you to look after Pat," Jake said. "He might be a bit slow, but he's a good man. Better than any of the rest of us at any rate."

That wouldn't be difficult.

Still Frank kept his peace. He liked this man, and talking to him would come easy. He saw something in Jake that he saw in the mirror when he shaved; something had been lost in both of them, and both were still trying to find it again. But he couldn't talk about it.

Not yet, and maybe not ever.

Jake stared out at the night for a while before continuing.

"I heard splashing down at the creek earlier. It could be that thing ain't dead yet. Or it could be there's more of the critters. Keep your wits about you," he said, and clapped Frank on the shoulder. "And whatever you do on the morrow, don't be letting the big man near a weapon. He ain't the best shot I've ever seen, and he's as liable to hit you as anything else."

Jake left Frank alone with the dark and the soft trickling of water in the creek. The air was chill, steam rising from the horses flanks, but Frank's deerskin jerkin kept the cold at bay for now.

The sound of Jake settling down to sleep slowly faded until all was silent. Frank let the quiet fill him. He took out his tobacco pouch and lit a pipe, savoring the taste of the hot smoke.

Inwardly he was still coming to terms with the earlier events.

The Pastor could have killed me.

Maybe he should have.

He had no idea why he'd stepped in front of the gun, beyond the fact that he'd seen too many young men die needlessly.

Hell, I don't even like the boy.

But not liking someone was no excuse for letting them get shot for being young and stupid. And now he was left with the consequences. He was to be a babysitter, both to Strang and Big Pat.

How the hell am I going to look after them. I can hardly look after myself most days without a drink.

He'd eyed the whiskey bottle all evening. When Pat went to sleep he'd even gone and stood beside it. But he hadn't touched it. It was a pledge he'd made to himself when he took this job.

This one I do dry, or not at all.

He'd kept that promise for three weeks now, but each day it got a little bit harder; each day the bottle called a bit louder.

A shadow crossed the moon, too fast to register its shape, but high overhead an eagle called out to its mate. It was as mournful a sound as Frank had ever heard. He looked up at the dark hills that loomed over the settlement and shivered.

He was a long way from finding peace.

Chapter 7

Jake went up the hill with the Pastor and the Squire just after sun-up the next morning.

His head pounded. He hadn't been able to sleep for long, and had taken to the whisky during the Pastor's watch, hoping that the liquor would send the demons away, for a while at least.

I should have known better.

The sun gleaned off the snow and lanced straight into his brain. His mouth tasted like something small and furry had shat in it, and his guts roiled, threatening to come out one end or the other if provoked. He had forced himself to eat some gruel, hoping it would settle his insides down for a while.

So far, it ain't working.

They equipped themselves as well as they could for a climb through the mine but they had no idea what they might face, and all three of them decided on weaponry over anything else. Jake even considered taking Strang's Walker, but it felt too heavy in his hand, and was too slow to reload in a tight spot. He stuck to his Colt, but took advantage of the Pastor's offer of ammunition and filled a shoulder pack with over a hundred paper cartridges. He also carried his old army saber, and although it banged against his hip as they climbed, he felt reassured by its weight.

Twenty yards up he had to stop to catch his breath as his stomach flipped and threatened to show him the gruel. He turned and looked back. The devastation of the settlement looked even more pronounced from up here. The path of the flood was clearly marked on the ground and looking at it now, Jake was surprised that anything had survived at all.

Pat was tending to the horses, studiously avoiding looking in Jake's direction.

Parting with the big man had been hard. The man was distraught at being left behind.

But I can't put him in a danger I know nothing about. Pat might be all I have left.

"I'm gonna lose you too," Pat had wailed when Jake told him to stay with Collins "And I'm gonna be left all on my lonesome."

No amount of pleading that they would only be gone an hour would convince him otherwise, and he had refused to meet Jake's eye as they said goodbye. Jake had gone up the hill with a heavy heart.

While Jake had stopped the Pastor had climbed ahead like a man many years younger, and Jake had to hustle to catch up. The Squire lagged ten yards behind, his face already as red as his tunic before they were halfway to the mine.

It was initially hard work as they picked their way through muddy slush and fallen rock, but it only took five minutes to reach the wide shelf in front of the shaft. Jake only looked back once more, as they got to the entrance. Pat was still tending to the horses with his back to Jake. Frank Collins stood on the cabin porch, looking up at the mine. They waved, almost in time with one another. Jake was gratified to see that the Greyback cradled the Walker pistol in his right hand. He still wasn't sure about Collins. Desertion was a serious matter, no matter which side you fought for. It told Jake he would never really trust the man until they'd been tested side by side in a fight.

And maybe not even then.

Leaving him with Pat and the Strang lad was a gamble, but he needed the best shots, the most seasoned fighters, in the mine with him, in case of trouble.

I hope I've done the right thing.

Then again, if I have, it will be a first.

He put it to the back of his mind as he turned towards the mine entrance.

It was immediately obvious that most, if not all, of the floodwater had come this way. When Jake was here last, the walls had been neatly squared off and lined with timber. That had been back in the autumn. Now it looked more like a natural cave. The shoring wood had been washed away and the walls showed signs of having been scoured by a rush of water and rock.

Everything was covered in a thin layer of frost that crackled underfoot.

"A blasting accident? That's what you said?" the Pastor asked.

Jake nodded, distracted. He was trying not to think of the fate of any men caught in such a torrent of water and rock.

They lit the lamps they'd brought from the cabin. The Pastor and Jake headed in but the Squire hung back in the entrance, looking warily into the darkness ahead.

"How long will the oil we have last?" the Englishman asked.

"Several hours at least," Jake replied. "But if we ain't out of the shaft by then, we'll be lost, for it only goes a hundred yards into the hill."

But it went on for longer than that.

A long way longer than that.

When they reached the spot where the mine had originally ended the shaft turned into a cave proper. The rough-hewn entrance was ten feet wide and the cave inside climbed at a thirty-degree angle. At the base of the incline an arrow; as long as Jake's arm and made of small rocks, pointed up into the passageway.

I'll leave a trail as I go like we did at Granddaddy's place.

When they were lads George had always been laying trails; trails to treasure. Back then the treasure had been old bullet casings and rusty knives. Now George had hoped it was the real thing.

"At least we know they got this far," Jake said. "Come on. Let's see where this goes."

The Squire held back again. In the dim light from the lamps his face looked pale and drawn.

"This is no place for men to be; crawling about in the dark like rats."

The Pastor laughed.

"Even in darkness light dawns for the upright, for the gracious and compassionate and righteous man."

"Pastor," Jake said. "If I had a dollar for every quote of yours I understood, I'd have two dollars."

"In the kingdom of the Lord, the rich man is no better off than the poor man."

"See," Jake said. "There's what I mean. I'd still ain't got any more than two dollars."

He'd hoped the Pastor's laughter would improve the Englishman's mood, but when Jake and the Pastor strode towards the incline the Squire did not move.

"Come, or go," Jake said. "It makes no never-mind to me. But there's a mother lode in here somewhere. You ain't looking for the Pastor here to get your share, are you?"

The Squire had a look back the way they had come, then followed Jake up the slope.

"This gold is proving a mite trickier to procure than you promised us lad."

Jake did not reply.

You ain't telling me nothing I don't know already Squire.

The walk up the passageway proved relatively easy. They had been climbing for nearly twenty minutes when Jake noticed a soft breeze on his face. It fell noticeably colder and wetter underfoot. Their footsteps took on a hollow, echoing quality that sounded almost like drums in the passage ahead of them.

"I've heard stories about mines," the Squire said. "Indeed, I remember one time in the Kalahari. It was hot as hell and..."

Jake tuned him out. The Squire liked to talk, but he didn't necessarily require an audience.

Minutes later they passed a side channel that led downwards. The rock around the entrance showed signs of recently having been sheared. The air around it felt damp and cold. There was a tang that Jake could taste at the back of his throat, like vinegar or piss. The noise of their footsteps echoed, as if the chamber opened out beyond the entrance into a larger space... a much larger space.

The Squire raised his lamp and investigated the entranceway.

"This hole is new," he said. "Another effect of the blasting maybe?"

He lifted a pebble and tossed it down inside. It clattered away into the depths. They never heard it hit bottom, although they listened for long seconds.

"I doubt anyone went that way," the Squire said after a while.

"Not voluntarily anyway," Jake replied.

As they walked away from the entrance Jake thought he heard a noise in the distance, a scrambling, scuttling sound. He stopped and listened, but the noise wasn't repeated.

The Squire and the Pastor were already up ahead. The Squire was now in the middle of yet another story, concerning a whore with a very large chest. The Pastor wasn't paying him any attention, but that never stopped the Englishman.

Several minutes later the Squire laughed uproariously at his own story. Meanwhile Jake managed only the merest sign of a smile, and the Pastor was as tight-lipped as ever. But they were able to douse the lamps as light came in from the far end of the cave.

"Wherever we are headed," the Pastor said. "It seems we are getting closer."

The going got soggy, and soon their boots tugged at cold wet mud. The last ten yards of the climb took as long as the previous hundred. The cave ended in a high lip they had to pull themselves over but finally they stood outside the mouth, caked up past the ankles in clinging mud.

It took Jake a minute to realize where they were; they stood in the bottom of a shallow basin, fifty yards across, full of damp mud and rotted weed.

He looked back at the hole behind them.

"It was a pond," he said, almost to himself. "And somehow our blasting collapsed this here hole, and emptied it."

The Pastor looked around.

"Sure looks that way," he said. "But look here. Do you think the blasting caused this?"

Tracks led away from the rim of the cave. There were many footprints of heavy work-boots. But overlaying them, following them, were even more of the deep gouge marks Jake had seen around the creek.

This is where the scorpion things came from? There are more of them?

The only way to answer that question was to climb out of the basin, and that proved to be more difficult than it looked.

They left the oil lamps by the cave mouth and began to slog their way through thick clinging mud. By the time they dragged themselves out onto firmer ground they were caked up to their thighs in clinging, damp goop. But the view that met them took away all thoughts of discomfort. .

They stood on a high rocky outcrop, looking down over a long glacial valley. It stretched off into the far distance, at least twenty miles long and two miles wide. Tall conifers lined the slopes on both sides below high snow-covered peaks. A large lake lay on the valley floor beneath them, with grass and snow covered plains dominating the long stretch away to the west. Several herds of large animals grazed on the plains, but it was too far to make out detail. They could only be bison, Jake thought, but there was something about these animals that just felt *strange*.

He put it to the back of his mind.

Animals ain't important.

He studied the ground around them, and found what he was looking for. Someone wearing boots had walked here. Frozen tracks led away towards what looked like a deer track. He raised his head and followed the line of it. The thin path ran alongside a stream for several hundred yards then led along the northern slopes just above the tree line.

Jake headed towards the start of the track. He was almost there when he realised the others had not followed. They were staring at a point several miles away on the other side of the valley. A thin column of smoke rose high into the air from a series of caves on the tree line.

There's someone alive down there.

Chapter 8

An hour after the other three went up into the cave Frank Collins' day went bad.

It started when Eric Strang woke and threw up on the floor at his feet. Frank was out on the porch at the time, but he heard the sound loud enough, and soon the faint odour of it wafted out the door.

That's all I need.

Pat was still tending to the horses, and all was quiet. Frank risked going inside the hut. The smell immediately got *much* worse.

"Bastards," Strang shouted as soon as Frank entered. "Let me loose or I swear I'll bloody kill the lot of you. You ain't got no right tying me up like this."

Strang didn't look like he was in any danger. They'd taken the gag off him when he slept so that he wouldn't choke and now that looked like a good decision. Vomit was caked down the youth's vest.

Frank smiled grimly.

"It's a good job we tied you up then, isn't it?" he said. He showed Strang the Walker. "I was the one who saved you from getting your brains blown out last night. So don't be getting uppity with me lad. I ain't in no mood for it."

"Where are the rest of you bastards?" Strang shouted, but Frank was already on his way back out to the porch. "They've gone for the gold haven't they? I'll bloody kill you all."

Frank shut the door behind him, but the silence of the day was ruined. He could still hear the youth ranting even through the thick wood of the door. He got the workings together for a pipe and was thankful for the hot smoke dispelling the lingering smell of the puke. But he wasn't given time to enjoy it.

One of the wagon horses pawed at the ground, gouging a groove in the damp grass. It tossed its head in the air and snorted loudly, the noise causing the other horses to prick up their ears.

Something's got them right spooked.

Frank checked, for maybe the fifth time that morning, that the Walker was fully loaded.

Pat hadn't yet noticed the rising commotion from the other horses. He was brushing down Jake's stallion, whispering in its ear as he stroked a hard brush along its flanks.

The horses tethered to the wagon whinnied. They tried to back away from the creek, pulling so hard that they dragged the wagon several feet through the mud before it came to a shuddering halt. A huge white claw came into view over the rim of the bank, *clacking* loudly as it opened and closed. Another rose up next to it, waving in the air, as if checking the surroundings.

Soon after, ten yards to the west, another pair of claws clacked as a second creature climbed out of the riverbed. A thick muscular tail curved over the squat body, the barbed tip hanging almost over the front end of the creature.

The horses stamped and kicked, high whinnying echoing in the hills above.

Big Pat looked around, confused. He went very still as he saw what was climbing out of the creek.

"Pat," Frank shouted, the clay pipe falling unnoticed from his lips. "Get back here. Now."

Pat didn't answer. He looked at the cabin, then at the horses. Even before he spoke Frank knew what the big man's decision would be. Pat moved to stand between the horses and the creek, weapon-less save for the hairbrush in his hand.

"Pat!" Frank called, pleading. But the big man stayed where he was.

"Get away from them animals," Pat shouted. "I ain't gonna tell you twice."

Frank ran forward, pulling out his Colt as he went. The Walker was in his left hand, but too heavy to wield while running. He raised the lighter weapon. But he could already see he would be too late. The beasts had both turned towards where Pat stood.

And they would reach the big man first.

Frank raised the Colt, but Pat was in his line of sight, and even pointing the gun in that direction almost struck Frank immobile.

"Pat. Get the hell out of the way."

Pat did the opposite. He walked forward until he could almost touch the creatures. He spoke to them, calmly, as if explaining something to a child.

"You ain't getting the horses," he said. "So you can forget that. Get back down that creek where you belong."

Claws clacked angrily. Two large tails waved in the air, arcing above Pat's head, swaying from side to side in long lazy sweeps. The big man ignored them.

"I done given you fair warning," he said. "If you come on, I'll send you to join your friend from last night, just see if I don't."

Frank was still several yards away when the tails bent backwards in the air. He'd seen almost the exact same movement before, in snakes.

They're getting ready to strike.

He had to make a quick decision. He went for the left, aimed and fired in one movement. He had fired too quickly and his aim was off. He missed by some distance. But it got Pat's attention.

The big man turned – a look of puzzlement on his face.

"You done shot at me Frank. What you go and do that for?"

Frank threw himself at Pat just as the beasts struck, grabbing him at the middle and wrestling him to the ground. The two men fell aside. The tails struck the ground with loud thumps. They hit almost exactly where Pat had stood a second before.

Frank rolled onto his back, bringing the Colt up, expecting an attack.

It didn't come. The beasts ignored the men and headed straight for the horses.

Pat was already pushing himself up.

"Now look what you've gone and done," he said. Before Frank could stop him he was up and running, once more heading straight for the creatures.

The horses snorted and whinnied, kicking out at the wagon, and at each other.

A muffled shout came from inside the cabin.

"Hey. What's going on out there?" Strang shouted. "What's all that commotion?"

One of the creatures turned and started to head towards the hut. The other kept going towards the horses.

Sound. They hunt by sound.

The horses went wild as the creature approached them, stomping and rearing, their whinnies and snorts filling the air with noise. Claws clacked eagerly and the muscular tail swished back and forth as it scuttled across the muddy ground.

It had almost reached the horses when Pat caught up with it. He grabbed the tail with both hands. The beast swung the tail violently from side to side, lifting Pat from the ground at each end of the swing. The big man held on tight. At the low point of the tail's arc he was able to dig his heels into the mud and pull. He was doing just enough to keep the clacking claws away from the horse's legs.

The other beast reached the cabin door. It tore frantically at the wood with its claws. Strang wailed... a wordless cry of fear that carried high into the night. Splinters flew in the air and wood cracked like gunfire. Strang wailed louder. The beast gouged ever harder at the door.

Frank decided that the door would hold longer than Pat's grip on the tail. He ran to the big man's aid. When the beast swung Pat to one side he fired the Colt.

The recoil sent a jolt all the way up his arm, but the shot blew a hole the size of a small plate in the shell. The tail suddenly lost some of its strength and Pat got his feet firmly on the ground. The big man wasted no time. He put his back into it and dragged the scorpion backward, leaving a deep track on the grass.

The creature scuttled around, turning in a tight circle in less than a second, away from the horses – but facing Frank.

The claws reached for his face. Frank got a good close look at the razor sharp serrated edge before he put another shot into the body, aiming for where he guessed the eyes would be.

The beast didn't slow. A claw clacked less than an inch from Frank's nose. He leapt aside, rolling and firing the Colt in the same movement to put another shot into the side beside the left front leg.

The leg blew apart and the beast lurched over, almost falling to the ground before righting itself, but it had given Pat time to make a move. He heaved the creature upright, showing Frank its belly.

Frank put two more shots into where he thought the brain might be. Bits of shell and viscous liquid flew. The air was suddenly full of an acrid stink like a wet cow pat on a hot day. Thick yellow fluid poured from the bullet hole.

"Shoot it again Frank," Pat shouted.

The Colt clicked down empty. He dropped it aside and raised the Walker, struggling with the weight of the weapon. He put a shot from the Walker near the last one from the Colt. The hole it blasted was as large as a dinner plate. The beast's innards started to leak through it, yellow-green organs glistening obscenely as they slithered to the ground. Frank saw Pat lean to one side to throw up. But he didn't let go of the beast.

"Again Frank," Pat shouted.

Frank shook his head.

"You can let it go Pat. It ain't going nowhere."

Pat dropped the beast. It fell with a wet thump to the ground and lay still.

Frank's heart thudded in his ears and his breath came in hot hitches.

"Well, that weren't too bad now, were it?" Pat said, putting out a hand to help Frank up. "Is it deaded?"

Frank kicked the shell. Then again. There was no movement.

"I guess so big man. But I ain't never killed nothin' like this before, so I can't be exactly sure."

At the same moment there was a crash.

Shit. I forgot the other beast.

The cabin door fell in. The second beast headed straight for where Strang sat screaming, still bound to the chair. The scorpion lifted the door in one claw and tossed it aside as if it was a piece of paper. Its tail hit the door-jamb on the way through. A fine spray of poison fell all around it.

Strang screamed louder. The claws clacked eagerly.

Frank started to run. He brought up the heavy pistol, but he couldn't guarantee not hitting Strang, and at this range, a shot from the Walker could kill a man outright. He was just going through the door when the beast reached Strang.

The youth threw himself backward, toppling the chair to the floor with a crash. The beast lunged, claws closing on the wood of the chair's legs and crunching them to kindling in a second. Strang screamed again, howling like a teething babe.

The claws clacked, loud as whiplashes.

"Help me for pity's sake," Strang squealed. "Get me out of this fucking chair."

The right claw reached towards the sound of his voice.

He screamed louder.

"For pity's sake, keep quiet," Frank said.

But Strang kept screaming.

Frank threw himself along the full length of the beast, grabbed at the left claw for balance, and put two shots into the area where he'd done so much damage to the one outside. Bits of shell and gore flew. The beast bucked but Frank held on tight and pulled the trigger again, and again.

Finally it clicked down empty.

The beast wasn't nearly finished. The left claw crushed the last remains of the chair to pieces and closed on Strang's right ankle. There was a loud snip. The foot fell away as steaming blood sprayed in an arc over the beast. Frank tasted it in his mouth and almost gagged.

Strang screamed and kicked, with both legs. The stump flailed and the air filled with more blood spray as Strang tried to struggle upright. At the same moment the beast brought its tail round. It hit the side of the youth's head with a wet slap. The barbed tip lodged in his neck just above the shoulder and stuck there. The tail swung to one side, dragging the screaming youth across the room. He left a trail of blood behind him.

Frank rolled off the shell into a crouch. Strang squealed like a stuck pig.

"Help me Jesus. Help me."

I don't think he's listening son.

Frank started to move forward, looking for an opening, intending to use the pistol as a club.

Pat had other ideas. Frank hadn't seen the big man since the cabin door fell open, but Pat had used the time well. He ran screaming into the room brandishing a large wood axe.

With one swipe he cut the flailing tail in two.

Strang fell heavily to the ground, taking the end of the tail with him. The other half sprayed gouts of yellow-white fluid around the room as the beast scurried frantically in all directions, looking for escape from this new threat. Pat weaved past the swinging tail and jumped onto the beast's back. He swung the axe, first to the left and then to the right. Pieces of shell and gore fell in chunks. The smell was almost too much to bear.

"Die," Pat shouted, "Die. You killed my horse you son of a bitch. Die."

Finally, it did. Its legs gave way beneath it and it collapsed with a wet muffled thud.

The room went quiet apart from the heavy hissing of the men's breath. Frank's chest felt tight with tension, and he had to force his hand to relax to let go of the pistol.

Strang moaned.

He's still alive. But only just.

The barbed tip of the tail stuck in his neck. The skin around the wound had already turned red and inflamed. His eyes rolled up showing white. A foamy mix of blood and spittle bubbled at his lips. The flow of blood at his ankle had slowed to a viscous trickle but there was enough blood on the floor to tell Frank the prognosis wasn't good. . He'd seen enough dying men to know there was little hope.

Big Pat still stood over the creature, hacking and slashing until there was little left but a pool of thick liquid and parts of broken claw and shell.

The tail part that was stuck in Strang's neck twitched. Pat hit it with the axe, again and again until it too was still.

Frank put a hand on Pat's shoulder as the big man raised the axe again.

"Enough Pat," he said softly. "Let's get the lad out of this charnel-house and see if we can do anything for him."

Strang started to convulse, the foam at his mouth becoming more blood than spit, his one remaining foot drumming hard on the floor.

With Pat's help Frank dragged the youth out to the cleaner air on the porch, but by the time he bent to try to stem the blood flow in the leg, Strang was dead; pale eyes staring, unseeing, at the sky.

Not again. Please Lord, not again.

Frank stood and walked away.

He was back at the field of Shiloh, with powder smoke in his nostrils, the taste of blood in his mouth and dead men that he should have protected behind him.

I did it again. I failed them again.

Tears coursed down his cheeks but he didn't notice. His head was full of the sound of screaming and gunshots; the sight of dead eyes and blood. He could see and hear nothing else.

He might have kept walking if Pat hadn't tugged at his arm.

"Frank? You okay, Frank?"

Pat pulled Frank round to face him. At first Frank only saw Strang's dead eyes staring back, but the hurt and confusion on the big man's face brought Frank back to reality.

Pat was wide eyed, and looked close to panic.

"What are we gonna do now Frank? What are we gonna do?"

Frank forced the despair away. He knew it would be back.

It always comes back.

He put an arm round Pat's shoulders and spoke quietly.

"You go and see to the horses Pat. They need calming. The smell of death is putting a fright into them."

Hell, it's putting a fright into me.

Pat calmed noticeably, his eyes clearing at the very thought of the horses.

"I can do that," he said, persuading himself. "Yep, I can do that." His eyes took on a pleading look that Frank had only ever seen before in a scared dog. "Just don't make me go back in the cabin, Frank. Please, say you ain't gonna make me go back in there?"

"I promise," Frank said. "You go see to the horses. I'll see to the cabin."

Pat turned to head for the wagon, but Frank stood for a long time looking at the cabin, and the dead body lying near the door. Several minutes passed before he could make himself walk.

Strang's dead eyes watched, accusingly, until Frank bent and closed them.

Ain't got no pennies, son. But I doubt you're going anywhere where you'll need them.

He took one look inside the hut. The creature's fluids were already starting to harden, forming a thick crust overlaying the blood spray. The smell brought gorge to Frank's throat and he backed out fast. The last thing he spotted was the amputated foot, still with a boot on, lying in a pool of blood and gore under a broken chair.

He stepped back out onto the porch, and gulped air until he felt he could breathe without throwing up.

"You okay Frank?" Pat asked again from over by the wagon.

Frank waved him away.

He looked over at the wagon, then up at the cave mouth on the hill.

Keep walking Frank, a voice in the back of his mind said. But something had hardened in him. Maybe it was killing the beast that did it, or maybe it was just that the bloody foot had thrown him over the edge of what he was prepared to suffer.

"Get some provisions together, Pat," he shouted. "We're heading up the hill to give Jake a hand."

Chapter 9

Jake found tracks along the side of the stream; not made by men, but by more of the scorpions. The tracks both ascended and descended from the dried pool above. They followed it for a hundred yards. The tracks followed the course of the stream. By the time the deer track veered away the three of them were leaving the only visible marks on the slushy snow.

The beasts don't move far from water. It was the same at the creek.

"Let's take the high road," he said. "We don't want to meet any more of them scorpions if we can help it."

"Amen to that brother," the Squire said. The Pastor gave the Englishman a disapproving look that did no good at all.

Jake kept his eyes on the thin column of smoke. It came from a dark cave mouth and he hoped against hope that one of the settlers, maybe even George, would appear there and wave cheerfully up at them.

But I gave up believing in fairy stories back in Nevada.

Down below on the valley floor a spiralling column of eagles soared, catching a thermal as the sun began to warm the air. They came up the side of the cliff slowly. It was only as the birds rose to almost eye-level that Jake realized how big they were. These were no mere eagles. Each wing was longer than the Pastor was tall.

Much longer.

Not only that, they were near as wide as any of the cabin doors back down at the Creek. Jake estimated the wingspan at fourteen feet, and some of the birds joining the spiral below looked to be even bigger still.

He watched the first bird as it rose above him. Its head was as big as two fists put together and even from a distance the beak was a formidable weapon, gleaming like a well-honed knife. The feathers at the tips of the wings looked as long as Jake's arm as they splayed to catch variations in the thermal.

There were now twelve birds soaring in the spiral, with more joining at the bottom of the thermal as they watched. The highest bird was already twenty yards above them, its shadow racing across the snow-field.

"Have you ever seen anything like it," Jake whispered.

"Well actually," the Squire said. "In Egypt they have vultures that can carry off a horse. I once saw…"

The Pastor interrupted him.

"Squire?"

"Yes?"

"For once, just shut the fuck up. And head for the trees. We're in trouble."

Jake turned towards the Pastor but the big man had already made a run for the tree line, plowing through the knee-deep snow. Jake saw why less than a second later.

A black shape swooped from high, coming at such a speed that he barely had time to react. He threw himself aside at the last possible moment and felt the wind from the bird's wings waft against his face. The attacking eagle screeched in frustration, talons raking the air where Jake had just been. It skimmed the ground, sending up a flurry of pow-dered snow and stayed just airborne enough to clear the trees at Jake's back. It banked off over the cliff edge, losing height as it lost the ther-mal.

A second bird headed for the Squire, but the man had seen it com-ing. The Englishman already had his rifle raised and was sighting along the barrel.

"Squire. Get down," Jake shouted. "This ain't no turkey shoot."

The Englishman stood his ground as the bird, wings tucked close to its body, talons outstretched, powered towards him.

If it hits him he's a goner.

The eagle closed to less than ten yards. The rifle boomed. The bird's head flew apart in an explosion of blood and feathers. Momentum kept the rest of it going. It tumbled to the ground, bones snapping like matchsticks. The body landed in a tangle of broken wings at the Squire's feet.

The Englishman turned and smiled at Jake.

"I do believe I may be the first man to bag a Thunderbird," he said, and laughed. "Just wait until I tell the chaps in the billet about this one."

Jake caught a glimpse of a black shadow moving swiftly across the snowfield.

Another eagle swooped from above towards them. Jake ducked reflexively.

Two shots rang out, and the eagle fell from the sky to land less than five yards from the other.

The Pastor stood, just inside the trees, twin pistols smoking in his hands.

"Now will you two gentlemen hurry?" he shouted.

Jake got up and in a stumbling run made for the trees. The Squire, laughing loudly, ran alongside.

"I have never had so much fun with my breeches on," the Englishman shouted as they made it under cover. "What a fine tale this will make."

They had made it to shelter just in time. Above them eagles screeched and swooped, talons raking the treetops and raining needles down on the cowering men.

"What in Hell are they?" Jake said.

The Pastor smiled.

"No need to invoke that place lad," he said. He started to quote again, "And God created the great creatures of the sea and every living and moving thing with which the water teems, according to their kinds, and every winged bird according to its kind. And God saw that it was good."

"According to its kind? And what kind are these?"

It was the Squire who replied.

"The large kind I should imagine." He brushed a patch of bloody feathers from his tunic. "Did you see that shot of mine? I imagine such a shot has rarely, if ever been attempted. Indeed, as I said earlier, I may be the first man to kill one of these creatures. It's a pity I have no proof. Maybe we can return this way for a feather or a beak even. Did I tell you of the time…"

Jake and the Pastor spoke in unison.

"Squire. Shut the fuck up."

Once the Squire stopped talking Jake noticed that it had fallen quiet.

Jake looked around. The eagles still circled above, but had stopped swooping at the trees above them, for the moment at least. Jake watched them warily for several minutes until he was sure they had lost interest.

"So what now gaffer?" the Squire asked. "It seems the deer track is well known to the predators. It might not be a good idea to continue on that course."

Jake had already made up his mind.

"We need to check who has made that fire. We go down."

And hope the cover of the forest holds.

Chapter 10

Frank and Pat were about to enter the mine when they heard the pop of weapons in the distance. They looked at each other.

"Sounds like trouble," Frank said. "Are you ready for this big man?"

Pat nodded, but he looked scared. In truth Frank was glad of the shots, for they gave him an excuse to cajole Pat along. It had been hard enough getting him to leave the horses.

"We'll set them loose," Frank had said. "They ain't stupid beasts. They'll be able to keep themselves from harm."

Pat hadn't been convinced, but he had smiled when the freed horses immediately ran off, putting as much distance between themselves and the creek as possible.

I only hope we can find them again when we need them.

Frank had another struggle when he tried to get Pat up to the mine.

"I don't like it," Pat had said petulantly. "It's dark. I ain't very good in the dark Frank."

So Frank had found them a pair of kerosene lamps in the store, and when he handed Pat the long wood-axe the big man actually smiled.

"That's better. I ain't any use with a gun no-how. You'll look after me Frank, won't you? You done promised Jake."

"I done promised Jake," Frank agreed.

And now I've promised myself.

And now the sound of the shots seemed to have firmed Pat's resolve.

"Best git gitting,"the big man said. "Sounds like there's gunplay up there. And that ain't hardly ever a good idea."

They lit the lamps and walked into the cave.

Frank had considered bringing Strang's Walker. It did an impressive amount of damage, but it was too heavy, took too long to reload and you had to lug a lot of ball and powder around with you. It was useful if you had plenty of time, and a horse to do most of the heavy carrying for you. That wasn't the case here. They had to travel light.

Frank carried his service rifle, and wore a Colt pistol in a shoulder holster. He had a bandoleer across his chest for the rifle bullets, and a small haversack with two boxes of dead men for the Colt. He let Pat carry a rucksack full of beef jerky, hard tack and two skins of water.

I hope it's enough.

Pat was nervy for the first fifty yards in, but he soon got used to the flickering light from the lamp. After a while the big man started to whistle to himself and Frank allowed himself to relax slightly. By the time they arrived at where the blasting had opened up the new tunnel Pat was the one eager to hurry on ahead.

"They went this way Frank," Pat said, pointing at the tracks on the ground. "This way."

The big man hurried ahead up the slope. Frank had to up his pace to keep him in sight. He only caught up fifteen minutes later to find Pat standing in front of a cave that led off the main tunnel. Pat looked worried again.

"I done heard something Frank," he whispered. "In there."

Frank took out his pistol. Holding the lamp ahead of him, he peered in to the cave. A cold breeze came up out of it. Something glistened on the wall and he turned to look closer.

A clump of silver globes hung there, reflecting his lamp back at him. They pulsated, almost as if they were breathing. Frank leaned closer.

"Be careful," Pat said sotto voce behind him, the sound sending a whispering echo through the cave. Frank became aware he was standing on the edge of a deep drop and carefully moved back a step.

He was still close enough to get a good look at the globes. What he saw sent a chill up his spine.

Eggs.

Small, perfectly formed scorpions squirmed inside balls of fluid held together by a thick gray slime. Frank felt the urge grow to rip and tear at them, to send them down into the cave below. But they were just out of reach and he wasn't about to risk falling into the dark.

"What is it," Pat whispered. "Is it a beastie?"

It's a beastie right enough. It's a whole lot of beasties big man.

But Frank said nothing. He pulled back to the main tunnel.

"Ain't nothing but the wind Pat," he said, putting his pistol away.

"Just the wind."

Pat didn't look convinced.

"You'll look after me, won't you Frank?" he said, almost pleading.

Frank didn't trust himself to speak. He just nodded and led them further up the tunnel.

They came out into the light a few minutes later, blinking as their eyes adjusted. They found the lamps where the others had left them, and put their own down alongside. It was easy to find where they had gone; their tracks showed as fresh gouges in the mud.

Neither of them enjoyed the muddy scramble that followed, and Frank felt relieved to feel wind on his face as they pulled themselves out of the basin and on to the rocky ledge above the valley.

Frank had half expected to meet the other men heading back, but there was no sign of them. Muddy footprints showed the direction they had probably headed. When Frank looked along the line all he saw was two dark and bloody masses on the snow.

We're too late.

"Jake!" Pat cried, and set off at a run.

Frank followed him down the deer trail, fearing the worst. He caught up just short of the nearest body. Pat had stopped, standing perfectly still, unable to move any closer. Once more the big man had tears streaming down his face.

"Not Jake," he cried. "Please, not Jake."

Frank walked over, and almost laughed as he got close enough to identify the body.

"It ain't Jake big man. Not unless he's grown wings since this morning," he said. He knelt and held up a bloody mass of bone and feathers. "They're birds. Big birds."

And I reckon we now know what all the shooting was about.

Now that he was down near ground level he could see the men's tracks heading towards the trees.

"Come on big man. They went this way. They can't have gone far."

Chapter 11

The descent through the trees seemed to take hours. Jake led the way. Several times he turned past a tree only to find that he stood over a sheer drop to the valley floor below. They had to retrace their steps twice, once for almost twenty minutes before they found a way down.

They caught occasional glimpses of the column of smoke on the far side of the valley and Jake got a clear view of the cave mouth several times. But they saw no signs of activity.

The frustration of not being able to get any closer to their destination was almost too much for Jake to bear. It didn't help that the Squire talked incessantly all the way down, reliving over and over the killing of the Thunderbird. By the time they did eventually reach the valley floor the bird had grown to gigantic proportions and the Squire had heroically saved both the Pastor and Jake from certain death.

Both Jake and the Pastor were already heartily sick of the tale, but Jake knew they would be hearing it for a long time yet.

Us, and every man the Squire ever meets in a saloon from now until Doomsday.

It was after noon when they finally walked out of the forest onto the valley floor. The sight that met them there quickly quelled any relief they felt at getting off the hill. The carcass of a large animal lay just beyond the trees. It had died some time ago, and most of the bones had been picked clean, but those that were left were strewn across a wide area. A huge skull lay in the slushy grass, empty eye sockets staring at them.

Bits of brown fur flapped in the wind, but there was nothing about the beast that Jake recognized. The rib cage was wide enough that two men could have walked inside it, and the thighbone was more than four feet long.

"Was it a bear?" the Pastor asked.

Jake shook his head.

49

"The teeth are all wrong. And it's too big to be bison. But I've no idea what it was."

"Well, once, in Africa," the Squire started, but one look from Jake put paid to that.

There were more tracks around the carcass. Jake was starting to recognize them.

"Them scorpion things again," he said. "They've been here too. Keep your eyes peeled. It ain't safe."

The tracks led to and from the stream that came down from the hill above. The stream fed into the large lake that sat at this end of the valley. Jake saw with a sinking heart that they were going to have to cross the water and skirt the lake if they were to reach the cave on the far side.

The Squire voiced what Jake was thinking.

"It's getting late gaffer," the Englishman said. "If we want to get back before dark, we need to get moving."

Jake nodded.

"I just need to see that cave. That's all. Once that's done, we'll head back. We'll return better equipped now we know the lay of the land."

The Squire and the Pastor looked like they wanted to argue the point but Jake didn't give them a chance. He strode towards the stream, looking for a place they might cross.

The closer he got to the water, the more bones he found. By the time he reached the bank of the stream the ground was covered, not just with bones, but with small chopped up pieces of fur and flesh.

The tracks of the scorpions were everywhere.

The Squire and the Pastor came to stand beside him.

"I've seen this kind of thing before," the Squire said softly.

"If this is another load of hogwash…"Jake started, but the Englishman waved him away.

"No, this is straight up."

The Squire couldn't take his eyes off the bones. "In the Hindu Kush there was a tiger there that kept to one area. It used to kill its prey near water sources. It would tear the prey to pieces and carry what it could away to feed its cubs. What was left behind in the course of a season looked like a bone-yard. Indeed, it looked a lot like this."

"What's a tiger?" Jake asked.

"You've seen a mountain lion?"

Jake nodded.

"Like that, but three times bigger."

Jake snorted.

"I knew it was hogwash."

Jake turned away, but not before noticing that the blood had drained from the Squire's face, and he was looking at the scattered bones with something that looked like fear.

"What do you say Pastor?" Jake asked. "Is there such a beast as the Squire describes?"

There was no reply. The Pastor stood over a pile of bones, moving them around with his feet. He bent, and lifted a leather belt, and then a work boot. The partially decomposed remains of a foot were still inside it.

"I believe we may have found at least one of those we are seeking."

The Squire bent and lifted a hat, then stepped back suddenly and threw up.

I don't want to see. Jake thought. He walked over and looked down. Bill Jackson's face stared up at him. Almost half the left side of the skull was caved in. The face was green and rotting with corruption.

But it's Farting Bill all right. I'd recognize that moustache any-where.

For several seconds Jake thought he'd be joining the Squire in losing the oatmeal they'd had for breakfast, but when he finally managed to drag his view away, all he felt was anger.

"There's another over here," the Pastor said softly. "Although there is not enough of him left for you to tell who they were. This is no way for Christian men to be laid to rest."

I doubt whether Christ has ever been heard of in this valley.

Jake turned his gaze back to where wisps of smoke still rose from the cave.

"I'm more determined than ever. We've found three. That's all. The others may still be alive."

He headed for the stream once more, drawing his pistol.

"I aim to have a look in that cave over there. You coming?"

The Pastor and the Squire looked at each other then followed close behind.

The stream proved to be shallow and easy to cross, though the water was bitterly cold. It soon seeped through inside Jake's boots. He squelched across the grassy area around the side of the lake.

There were more bones and pieces of decomposing flesh scattered everywhere near the shore. Jake forced himself to look at them all. None looked human but in most cases there was too little left to be sure.

After a mile Jake noticed the remains of some structures in the lake, timber platforms that had once been huts of some kind, but now destroyed. As he got closer he could make out the now tell-tale gouges in the wood and the track-marks in the mud along the shore.

Someone else lived here. They lived here, then the scorpions came.

There was something about the structures that seemed strange to him, but he couldn't figure out what it was. He didn't have time to think about it. He looked ahead at the cave that was now little more than a mile away. Something moved in the cave-mouth, something that stood on two legs.

They're still alive!

Jake broke into a run.

Chapter 12

Frank and Pat were lost.

Somewhere on the way down the hill they had wandered from the tracks they had been following and now they trudged through almost knee deep snow along a high ridge, heading back almost the way they had come.

Neither of them had spoken for several minutes, just walking with their heads down, watching their steps. Frank was surprised when Pat shouted.

"We're clear. Look. There's a stream."

They were indeed clear, but Frank's heart sank.

We've gone in a circle.

They were back at the side of the stream that led down from the high outcrop. A hundred yards or so above them the black bodies of the large eagles still lay strewn on the ground.

"What are we going to do now Frank?" Pat asked. "What are we going to do? We done been walking for hours and we ain't got nowhere."

Frank studied the side of the stream. There was a path of sorts there, thinner than the one they had originally followed above the tree line, and one that dived alarmingly steeply down the hill.

But a path nonetheless.

"It's up to you big man," Frank said. "Do you want to go back to the Creek?"

Pat's eyes went wide.

"No sir. We done came to find Jake. He's down there somewhere."

Frank looked at the stream path once more.

"Okay big fella. Down it is. Stay close behind me," he said. "And put your feet where mine have been. We'll take it slowly. And yell at me if it gets too scary for you."

Pat nodded. He looked frightened again, but there was something else there that Frank was glad to see. It was determination.

Frank led them down. At first the descent proved relatively easy. He had a bad moment when his foot slipped and he almost tumbled, but Pat grabbed him by the arm and kept him from tumbling down the slope on his arse.

"Don't worry Frank," Pat said. "I'll look after you."

They were both laughing as they headed down the next part, but went quiet when the track got so steep that they had to put hands against the frozen ground to keep their balance.

Things got worse when they came to a lip and the stream tumbled over into a waterfall.

Frank inched forward towards the edge.

"Hold my belt Pat. I need to get a good look to see our way."

The drop was only four feet, but that wasn't what got Frank worried. The waterfall fed into a pool on a ledge. Bones and pieces of meat lay both in the water and around the edges. Frank saw immediately what had happened; the beasts brought their food this way, and pieces of it had been dropped and discarded as they scrambled up over the lip where Frank stood.

It's like a damned abattoir.

"Okay Pat. We're going down. There are some bones and meat and stuff down there. Just keep your eyes on my feet and follow me."

"No beasties?" Pat said quietly, the fear back in his eyes. "You're sure there ain't no beasties?"

Frank clapped him on the shoulder.

"No beasties big man. Just dead meat. And the quicker we move, the quicker we'll get past it. Come on."

Frank lowered himself over the lip. He had to get his legs in the water to swing down onto the ledge below and gasped as the cold gripped him. Pat followed quickly behind. Frank saw that the big man had his eyes screwed shut as he came down. He took Pat's hand.

"It's okay Pat," he said softly. "Let me lead you. We'll get you past it."

Tears leaked from the corners of Pat's scrunched up eyes.

"I'm sorry Frank," he said. "I guess I ain't no more than a big baby."

But he still didn't open his eyes.

Frank started to pick his way through the gory mess on the ledge. Some of the parts were near as big as melons. He wasn't about to tell Pat, but one looked suspiciously like a human thigh torn roughly from a hip.

Frank reached the edge of the ledge and saw with relief that the path was a lot less steep from here on down. His gaze followed its curve all the way to the valley floor. Three men stood beside the lake down in the distance.

"I see them Pat," Frank said.

He didn't get an answer from Pat. The big man was looking over to their right.

Something growled in the trees. The pine needles rustled.

Frank never got time to react. He turned just as it pounced on him. He only had time to register that it was huge, reddish orange and shaggy before it hit him. He still had hold of Pat. The big man's grip tightened on Frank's hand.

All three of them rolled away down the slope in a spray of snow.

Chapter 13

Jake was fifty yards from the cave.

He'd had no more sightings of anyone there, but his mind was full of hope and expectation. What he hadn't been expecting was the spear that flashed past his head. A second plunged into the ground at his feet.

"Get down man," he heard the Squire yell. "We're under attack."

Jake's army training took over. He threw himself onto his belly and got his pistol out in front of him, sighting along the barrel to the mouth of the cave. They had no cover. The ground was almost flat and mossy, any grass no more than two inches long.

If anyone up there has a gun we're all goners.

Nothing moved.

The Squire crawled up next to him.

"Keep your head down lad. This isn't the first time I've been in this situation."

Another spear thudded into the ground near them. Jake was surprised by how small it was, but the stone head had been worked to a thin edge. It didn't matter what size it was.

If one of them hits, it's going to go right down to bone.

"We can't just lie here," Jake whispered. "Sooner or later one of us is going to get hit."

The Squire smiled. He seemed to be enjoying himself.

"The British Army trains for this kind of thing lad. Cover me."

Before Jake could argue the man fired six rapid shots from his pistol towards the cave mouth and squirmed forward on his elbows, moving as fast as a lizard on hot sand.

Jake send six more shots towards the cave. Two spears thudded down in the space between himself and the Squire, then all went quiet once more.

The Pastor edged up beside Jake as he reloaded.

"Have you seen anybody?" Jake asked.

The Pastor shook his head. He took out his pair of pistols.

"But you'd best get moving lad. If we lie here too long our nuts will freeze to the ground."

"Fine words for a Pastor," Jake said.

"No man that hath his stones broken shall come nigh to the offerings of the Lord," the Pastor said with a straight face.

"Now you're just making shit up," Jake replied.

The man in black smiled.

"Get thee hence lad," he said. "I'll cover you."

Jake started shooting. Both the Squire and the Pastor joined in. The shots echoed around the valley. A hail of spears replied. One of them landed six inches from Jake's nose. Another missed his left hip by less than that. But he reached the Squire's side safely.

The Englishman smiled broadly as Jake crawled beside him.

"Dashed un-welcoming behavior," he said. "Don't you think?"

Jake reloaded again from his shoulder bag. The paper cartridges felt slightly damp. He hoped that was just the moisture from his fingers.

Otherwise we're in real trouble.

The Squire finished loading his rifle.

"Twenty yards to go," he said. "Let's get the Pastor up here first, then we'll go for it."

Go for it?

"That's your plan? That ain't no kind of plan at all."

Once more the Englishman smiled.

"Elegant in its simplicity, don't you think?"

Jake and the Squire set up a covering fire as the Pastor squirmed across the gap towards them. More spears fell, but none got too close to them.

The Pastor crawled beside Jake.

"On three," the Squire said. "Then we head for the cave. The Pastor has the most firepower so he goes first and we back him up. Once inside we take the cave then establish a defensive perimeter."

The military talk proved strangely reassuring for Jake. It gave him focus, reminded him that he had been in tight spots in the past and came out by working with the others of his team.

We can do this. I have to do this. George might be in that cave. So might the others.

They waited while the Pastor reloaded his pistols. Jake raised his head several inches, risking a look at the cave. Still nothing moved, but no more spears came in his direction.

"On three," the Squire said. "One, Two…"

The Pastor went first. He ran forward in a crouch, swerving from side to side, guns blazing, the noise almost deafening. Jake backed him up as well as he could. He and the Squire followed behind and they covered the ground to the mouth of the cave in seconds.

He almost ran into the back of the Pastor. The man stood just inside the cave, guns raised and smoking. The man in black was not moving inside. Jake saw why when he joined him.

At first he only saw the children.

Hairy children?

He soon saw that his first impressions were wrong. These weren't children. Yes, they were small, but their features, even obscured by the shaggy hair that seemed to cover them from head to foot, were those of adults. More than twenty of them stood just inside the cave. All were armed with spears or stone axes.

And none of them was more than thirty inches tall.

Jake was so taken aback that it took him several seconds to see the man lying at their feet, bound and trussed like a turkey, two stone spears pressed at his neck with enough weight to draw trickles of blood.

The intent was plain.

Come any closer and we kill him.

The man was thin, almost skeletal, cheekbones showing as sharp edges through skin that was gray and translucent. His eyes had sunk deep back in their sockets, looking like black pools of despair.

But Jake would recognize him anywhere. He was too dazed to notice when the small people disarmed them of their guns. He still couldn't look away from the figure on the floor; the man who stared, eyes glazed and unfocussed, into a far distance.

George?

Chapter 14

The tumble down the snowy hillside seemed to go on forever.

Pat screamed all the way.

Frank still had no idea what attacked them. He got momentary glimpses, of a bright blue eye, of a curved tooth near a foot long and a huge paw with claws like knives. All Frank knew was that he clung to a handful of orange fur.

And if I let go I'll probably be dead in seconds.

Trees flashed past them. At any moment Frank expected to hit a tree or even a rock.

And that will be the end of that.

But, miraculously, they came to a halt, stopped by a long drift of snow. The orange beast snarled and jumped upright, so fast that Frank was left with some of its fur in his hand.

Frank stood, groggy and dizzy from the tumble.

Ten feet from him stood the largest cat he'd ever seen. He had once seen a mountain lion take a deer and thought that was impressive enough, but the creature that circled them now was bigger by far. Its body was ten feet long, held up by massive legs covered in the thick orange fur. The paws were as large as dinner plates and tipped with black claws. Muscles bunched along its shoulders and its shaggy coat rippled slightly in the wind. The furry tip of a long muscular tail swished behind it, but it was the front end that Frank focussed on.

If ever God made a pure killing machine, surely it looked like this.

Twin fangs hung over the lower jaw, each near a foot long. The beast salivated, dripping long ropes of stringy drool. Deep blue eyes stared fixedly at Frank. It purred, like a small kitten having its back scratched.

Frank was aware that Pat was still getting to his feet beside him.

"Are you okay big man?" he whispered.

The beast cocked its ears and studied them. Now that it had them cornered it seemed unsure as to what to do next.

Pat lifted the axe.

The cat looked at the weapon. It growled at them again, a rumbling sound that came from deep in its chest. It sounded like distant thunder.

"Easy, Pat," Frank said. "I think it's as scared of us as we are of it."

Pat laughed nervously.

"I ain't ready to put a bet on that Frank."

Neither am I big man. Neither am I.

Frank had lost the rifle somewhere on the tumble down the hill, but he still had the pistol. The beast watched, curious, as he drew it carefully from the holster. It didn't back off. And it didn't growl as it had when it saw the axe.

It has no fear of the weapon. It has never seen a firearm. That gives me an advantage.

Frank checked the weapon. It was fully loaded, but the gun felt damp. He could only hope that the cartridges had kept dry.

"What we do now Frank?" Pat whispered.

"I guess I'm gonna have to shoot it."

The beast circled them slowly. It opened its mouth and roared, the noise sending small birds flying skyward from the trees nearby.

Frank brought up the gun.

"If you're going to shoot it, do it now Frank," Pat said. "Before I pish my pants."

Before Frank could fire, a volley of shots rang out from the valley behind them. The beast roared again, and sprang straight at him.

Frank got one shot in, but it was rushed. He didn't see whether he'd hit it or not as he rolled aside. One of the beast's paws caught him on the left shoulder. It felt like being hit by a hammer. Claws dug deep, through Frank's jerkin and into his flesh. He had a sudden flash of ice cold pain, then heat as blood poured down inside his shirt. He rolled away fast, but when he brought up the handgun the barrel was full of impacted snow. He had no time to clear it. The beast was already turning back towards him.

"Run Pat," he shouted. "Get free while you can."

Once more the big man had other ideas. As he had done when protecting the horses, Pat stepped between the big cat and Frank.

"You ain't gonna have him," he said, raising the axe above his head. "I ain't gonna let you."

The cat rushed him. As if he'd been doing it all his life Pat stepped nimbly to one side as it reached him. He brought the axe down, hard. It bit deep into the beast's shoulder just behind the neck. Blood spurted.

The cat yelped in pain.

Pat roared, as loud a sound as any made by the cat. He ran straight for it, swinging the axe above his head.

The cat turned and fled. The last thing Frank saw was the furry tip of its tail flicking as it went into the trees. A line of blood traced its path in the snow.

Pat stood there, axe raised, waiting to see if the beast would return.

Frank's shoulder suddenly decided to become aware of the wound. The pain caused blackness to creep at the edges of his vision. He pushed himself upright, and then forced himself to smile as Pat turned back to him.

"You okay, Frank?" Pat said. Blood dripped thickly from the end of the axe in his hand.

"Thanks to you, big fella," Frank said. "I owe you one."

Somewhere nearby the cat roared in pain and anger.

"We need to get somewhere under cover," Frank said. "I've got a wound that needs binding. And yon kitty-cat might come back."

Pat's eyes went big as he looked at the torn cloth of Frank's jacket, and the blood seeping from beneath it.

"Are you sure you're okay Frank?"

Again Frank managed a smile, although in truth he was more tired than he'd been at any time since Shiloh.

"Let's find somewhere to rest," he said. "I'll feel better after a rest."

He walked towards Pat. He managed three shuffling steps. The blackness came at him in a rush.

"Frank!" he heard Pat shout.

Then he heard no more.

Chapter 15

Jake was still in shock as the small people herded the men inside the cave. He felt the points of several spears poke him in the ass with every step he took.

"You ever seen anything like these Squire?" Jake whispered.

A spear jabbed him in the buttock. Jake decided keeping quiet might be a good idea.

The small people jabbered among themselves, a high, almost sing-song language that was completely incomprehensible. Jake tried to make out any word he might recognize, but soon gave up.

They were marched through a large cave that was obviously the main living area. A small hearth contained the fire that they'd seen smoking. Straw and moss pallets served as the only bedding. Stones had been hollowed to serve as bowls for food, but there was no sign that these people knew anything at all about metal. The people them-selves were naked, apart from the fact that several of them wore neck-laces made of wood and bone.

And there ain't no sign of no gold neither.

The men were pushed through to the back of the main cave and into an alcove. They were poked and prodded with the spears until they got the message.

We're meant to sit.

Once they got down onto the ground the three men were swiftly and efficiently tied up, bound tight with stiff rope that looked to be made of coarse hair. Jake and the Squire still had their sabers, but their hands were tied so firmly there was no chance of reaching them. The small people left them alone in the near-dark. Just enough light reached this far into the cave for them to see each other's faces.

"Why didn't you shoot man," the Squire said to the Pastor. "We could have taken them all easily."

The Pastor took a while to reply. He seemed lost in thought.

"Ain't never shot a child afore," he said quietly. "And I ain't intending to start now."

"These are not children," the Squire said. "I've seen their like before..."

The Pastor snorted. "Save it Squire. We've all heard your tales."

"And some of them are even true," the Squire replied. "I may embellish some of the points from time to time... but some are indeed true. Four years ago I was in Africa, babysitting a mad Scotsman who was trying to bring Christ to the heathens. He failed, mostly, but that's beside the point. There are small people in the jungle there; pygmies they call them. They too all run around naked as the day they are born, and they are near as small as these. Not as hairy though."

"Hogwash," the Pastor said. "I know a child when I see one."

"They are not children," a hoarse voice said from across the alcove.

"George?" Jake said.

"Hello, Jake," the man replied, but there was no emotion in his voice, only a dull monotone.

"George. What happened to you? Where are the others?"

George began to talk, still in the same dull monotone.

Jake noticed that darkness was starting to fall outside, but soon he was lost in the story that unfolded.

Chapter 16

"I left you a note," George began. "And that's the last I saw of Ruby Creek. I ran up through that cave like the hounds of hell themselves were snapping at my ass. Not because I was afeared of what had happened to the rest. No. I was afeared they'd find the mother-lode afore I got there; afeared we'd lose our stake.

"I found them hacking away at a rock face up near the top of the cave. Somebody said that was where the seam ran, but I never saw it. The rest were convinced though. They attacked that wall like it led to a roomful of whores, a-scrambling and a-yelling. They were near to a fist-fight, and tempers were running high.

"That all changed when part of the roof caved in. Jim Forbes was first in. And he was first out. He held the stump of a hand up, blood spurting hot and dark all over us. He didn't get a chance to speak before the beasts came out of the cave behind him. A big fucking claw took his head off at the neck. That was enough for us.

"We scarpered.

"The way back down to the Creek was already cut off. The beasts were everywhere, crawling over each other, filling the tunnel, that fucking clacking echoing all around us like gunshots.

"I was the only one smart enough to have a weapon with me, but I used up all my ammo in seconds and didn't even slow them. We only just got out of the cave, with the fuckers snapping at our asses all the way.

"We lost four more men in that fucking mud. Chopped to little bits they were, and their screams were horrible.

"I'm not shamed to say it. We ran. Fast as we could. We jumped down that hill like fucking deer, the beasties at our heels all the way. At the bottom Farting Bill and a few others wanted to stand and fight, but the rest of us were too afeared. So we ran again, and if any of us heard the screams behind us, we didn't speak of it.

"We thought we were saved when we came to the lake huts. But that was just the start of our trouble. Those beasties kept coming down into the valley, a flood of the gray bastards, all snapping and crawling, killing their way through everything that got in their path and leaving nothing behind.

"And that included the people of the lake. Tens of them got chopped to meat before they knew what hit them. We all ran for the caves, prospectors and natives together. Thankfully the beasts ignored us. They had more than enough food down at the lake, and they don't seem over keen to move too far from the water.

"That first night, we were treated like guests."

George stopped talking as several of the small people came into the alcove carrying steaming bowls of food.

"I'd eat as much of it as you can," George said dully. "They only give us the same amount as they eat themselves. And that ain't enough to keep a man alive. Not for long anyway."

George coughed, and something rumbled deep in his chest, something that sounded broken. He wheezed, trying to breathe, and it took several minutes before he could speak. In that time the small people spoon-fed Jake, the Pastor and the Squire from the small bowls.

Jake got his first good look at them.

Although they were short, they did indeed look like tiny versions of perfectly formed adult humans, with everything in proportion. Back in his carnival days Jake had seen several short people in the geek shows.

But ain't none of them were ever near as hairy.

The hair seemed to cover everything apart from the flat faces and the palms of the hands. Jake suspected the soles of the feet would be the same. On the exposed areas the skin was thick and dark, like old weathered leather. Their eyes were blue and piercing, almost shining in the darkness of the cave. Their lips looked thin, blue and cold, yellow broken teeth showing behind them.

They showed no fear of the men as they used heavy stone implements to spoon the gruel into their mouths. It tasted like oatmeal and salt but smelled foul. Despite that, Jake did as George said and ate as much as they would give him. When they finished and had turned to leave, Jake looked back over at his brother. The man looked even paler than before.

He's as near death as any man I've ever seen.

"What's wrong with you George. What happened?"

George laughed bitterly.

"Winter happened." He coughed again, and blood bubbled at his lips. "Consumption happened. Ain't gonna take a doctor to tell me I'm fucked.

"As I said, that first night, we were treated like guests. But the food they gave us was drugged, and when we woke, we were trussed up like turkeys, like you are now. I've been in this fucking cold cave ever since, with the damp and the fleas and no grub fit for a grown man to eat."

He spat out a wad of blood that looked worryingly firm, and grimaced in pain.

Jake was almost afraid to ask the next question.

"And the others?"

George sobbed.

"Ain't no others. You are the others now."

Then he laughed.

He is insane.

That, more than anything else, frightened Jake, shaking him to the core. George had always been the strong one, the practical one. While Jake was running off, first to join the Joshua Potts Travelling Carnival, then later to enlist in the Army, George worked the farm, long after the land had nothing left to give. It was George who organized the disparate farmers enough for the journey to Montana, George who ordered the supplies and kept the food coming. Without George, none of this would have happened.

And with that thought, came the realization of what was really wrong with his brother.

Without George, none of this would have happened.

He blames himself.

Before Jake could say anything, George had gathered enough strength to continue.

"There were twelve of us left that first morning. At first we counted ourselves damned lucky to be even alive. The little fuckers kept us tied up though, and no amount of shouting at them would make them pay us any mind beyond feeding us. We wallowed in our own piss and shit for days on end with nothing to do but bitch at each other and feel sorry for our pitiful fucking selves."

He laughed bitterly.

"We soon came to miss those days."

George coughed again, hacking and spluttering.

"Rest man," the Squire said. "Your story can wait for another time."

George laughed again, long and hard.

"Wait? What do you think I've been doing these long fucking months? Needlework?"

That brought another bout of bloody coughing. When he spoke again it was almost a whisper.

"I done waited for you all winter Jake. Waited for my little brother to come and save me. Now you're here. And it's all too late."

"It ain't never too late, George. Hush now. Get some rest."

George continued as if he hadn't heard.

"It happens on rainy days mostly," he said. "You can hear it dripping, even back here, drumming on the stone in the mouth of the cave. We came to fear that sound."

He went quiet. Even in the rapidly dimming light Jake saw the tears glistening on his cheeks.

George spoke so quietly it was almost inaudible.

"They took Johnny Galbraith first. The boy cried for his mother, cried like a newborn babe. But they took no heed. They never take no heed.

"We heard their drums ten minutes later. Not long after that everything went quiet. We heard a rattling clacking, like distant gunfire. We all knew what it was, but no one spoke, not even when Johnny started to scream; such screams as you'll never hear outside Hell itself. Higher and higher they went, as if he was being torn apart piece by piece.

"Each of us could see it in our minds, and all of us wished we couldn't.

"Finally, mercifully, everything went silent. The hairy ones came back and they were happy, smiling, as if they'd just had a great victory."

George fell silent for so long that Jake thought he must be asleep, but he started again.

"Every rainy day after that they fed another of us to the beasts. Every rainy day they are happy."

"All of you?" Jake said, the horror of it only just starting to register.

George's head slumped forward and he started to weep.

"I prayed Jake. I prayed to be spared. And I thought I'd been answered. They took everyone but me. Then, this morning, I heard the shots. I really thought God had answered me. Please, forgive me. They all died because of me."

He wept inconsolably for a long time before falling silent.

Only then, sitting in almost complete darkness, did Jake hear the noise from the front of the cave.

It was the steady drip of rain falling on stone.

Chapter 17

Frank woke to a world of pain and darkness. At first he thought he'd gone blind, but as his eyes adjusted he realized that night had fallen. He tried to move but he was backed up, almost wedged, into a crevasse in a rock face. He had been stood upright, held up by the stone around him. He could only see forward to where a hunched figure sat over a small fire.

"Pat?" he said, but his voice came only as a throaty whisper. His mouth was dry and he couldn't make any spit to wet it. He tried again.

"Pat?"

This time the big man heard. He stood from the fire.

"You're alive Frank. Praise the Lord, you ain't deaded."

Frank pushed himself out of the crevasse. The pain at his shoulder flared. He was almost afraid to look at it, but when he did he saw it had been neatly bandaged with strips of cloth. He moved the shoulder. Pain flared again, but it didn't feel like anything was broken.

"I guess I'll live big man," he said. He took a step forward, staggered and nearly fell. Pat caught him and led him to the fire.

"Take it easy Frank. You done lost a lot of blood. I guess you'll be weak for a while, huh?"

"You guessed right, Pat."

Frank sat down hard and the world span around him. He felt as giddy as if he'd just chugged half a bottle of sour-mash.

And what I wouldn't give for one of them right now.

Pat handed him a water-skin and he took to that as gratefully as if it were whiskey. His hand shook and he got more water down his vest than in his mouth until Pat steadied his arm.

"Where are we, Pat?" he asked once he'd had his fill.

"I didn't know what to do," the big man said. "I thought you was deaded. All I could think of was to get you safe, so I carried you up here."

Frank's head felt steady enough that he could look round without feeling as if he would fall over. They sat on a high rocky ledge looking down over the dark valley. The valley floor was at least a hundred yards below.

"You carried me all the way up here?"

Pat nodded.

"You done said to find somewhere safe. I didn't know what else to do."

The big man looked like he might be about to cry.

Frank put a hand on Pat's shoulder.

"You did good big fella. You did real good."

Pat broke into a smile.

"I done patched you up too. Just like I learned from Grammy."

Frank tested the bandage. It felt tight and firm. A field doctor could hardly have done it better.

"Pat, you never cease to amaze me."

Pat handed him his haversack.

"I saved this. We got the food too... and your pistol... and the axe. I ain't found the rifle though."

Frank found his tobacco pouch and clay pipe in the bag and started putting a smoke together.

"You did just fine Pat. You did just fine."

Frank's shoulder throbbed with a deep heat as he leaned over to get the pipe going. He almost fell face first into the fire but managed to steady himself just in time.

I ain't going anywhere anytime soon. Best get used to the idea.

"The big cat? It's not been back?"

Pat's eyes narrowed.

"I done heard something earlier, something big in the trees below. But ain't nothing's come up here." He laid the axe across his lap. "And don't you worry none Frank. Ain't nothing going to harm you again."

Frank laughed.

"Wasn't I supposed to be looking after you, Pat?"

The big man didn't smile. He looked deadly serious.

"You need to get yourself right, Frank. Then you can look after me."

Frank sucked the first puff from the pipe and immediately his head felt light.

Maybe that wasn't such a good idea.

But he stuck with it, the taste of the tobacco grounding him and reminding him of places where unnaturally large cats didn't prowl and scorpion beasts couldn't kill you in seconds with a single sting.

What in God's name have we stumbled into here?

It started to rain, but Pat had chosen the spot for the fire carefully. A large overhang protected them from the worst of the elements.

Pat stared into space, and after a while started to sing quietly.

There's a good time coming, boys, a good time coming.

We may not live to see the day, but Earth shall glisten in the ray of the good time coming.

Cannonballs may aid the truth, but thought's a weapon stronger.

We'll win our battle with its aid, wait a little longer.

Frank had tears in his eyes when the big man finished.

"There is a good time coming, Pat. I promise."

He tried to stand but his legs wouldn't hold him up. He put the pipe down, slowly. His hand seemed to recede away from him into the far distance.

"I think I'll go to sleep for a while," he heard himself say. Darkness took him fast, and as he went down, big Pat's voice sang alongside him in the blackness.

There's a good time coming, boys, a good time coming.

Chapter 18

There was to be no sleep for Jake.

The fires from out in the main cave lent the alcove a red glow that was accompanied by the smell of cooking meat. Jake started to salivate, acutely aware that the gruel had only just taken the edge off his hunger. But no more food was brought to them. They sat alone in the flickering dark.

George slept fitfully, whimpering like a whipped dog, and once more Jake felt tears form that he could not wipe away.

"Talk to me, lads," he said to the others. "How are you holding up?"

"We are in a dark place gaffer," the Squire said. "Make no mistake."

The Pastor laughed.

"What Squire, no tales of how you evaded the grasp of the fuzzy-wuzzies while simultaneously bedding a whole harem of luscious virgins? Surely an army man of your caliber has a means of escape from our predicament?"

The Squire smiled broadly.

"Oh ye of little faith. Even now, I am working on a plan of action that will see us free of here and home in time for tea and tiffin."

This time Jake laughed.

"Best make it quick Squire. If George is right, that rain spells doom for one of us on the morrow."

"Weeping may endure for a night, but joy cometh in the morning," the Pastor said.

"Now that one I do understand," Jake replied. "But joy ain't in much supply around here right now."

"Maybe the others will come, when we haven't returned?" the Squire said.

The Pastor laughed again.

"A deserter, a hothead and a man with as much wit as a boy? Those are to be our saviors? Forgive me Squire, but I shall put my trust in the Lord."

"Yes," Jake said. "Ain't he doing well for us so far?"

The Pastor ignored him, and started to mouth prayers under his breath. With his hat off and his thinning hair showing, the older man suddenly looked less imposing, almost frail.

This cave could be the breaking of all of us.

The night crept by at a dead slow pace. The Pastor and the Squire eventually managed to find some rest, but Jake couldn't sleep. He kept seeing Farting Bill's face staring up at him. And when that faded, he saw the dead eyes of the poisoned horse back at the creek.

I ain't gonna end up like that. I'll kill myself first.

Late into the night George woke with a start. He seemed surprised to see Jake.

"Shit, Jake," he said. "I done been hoping you were just another dream."

"No such luck George," Jake said, trying to keep his voice light. "If I were you I'd be dreaming about other things. Womanly things, if you catch my drift."

George didn't smile.

"I been having a shitload of dreams lately," he said. "And ain't one of them been worth a fart."

Jake managed a thin smile back.

"Well maybe now that I'm here things will improve on that front. I just moseyed on down to see how my big brother was doing."

George tried to laugh but only managed a hacking cough that brought up more blood.

"There ain't much room for improvement. I'm a goner Jake," he said when he could muster enough energy. "My stomach hasn't stopped doing the Tennessee quick step for weeks now, and I can't hardly breathe without bringing up blood."

"I ain't gonna sit here and listen to quitting talk George."

George coughed again.

"I don't see as you've got any more choice than I do. In the morning, when they come for me, you ain't gonna make a fuss. I want you to promise me that."

"I ain't promising no such thing."

George spoke quietly.

Big brother is back.

"You have to Jake. You've got folks coming for you. You have to hope they get here. Like you came for me."

Jake started to cry. He let the tears come.

"I came to save you George. And did a piss poor job of it too."

"You can't save everybody Jake," George said. "I told you that once afore."

Jake remembered. Dying squaws, executed braves and murdered children lying naked in the mud; that was the legacy of his army years. He'd spoken up against it, and been court-martialed for his trouble.

You can't save everybody Jake

George had said that when Jake finally got let out of the penitentiary, just before they set out for Montana. Jake was lost in memory and only George starting another coughing fit brought him back.

"I done need another promise from you Jake," he said after a while. "These small folk here ... I'll be wanting you to promise to try to save them."

"Save them? After they done killed all my friends?"

"What we did killed more of them than they have killed of us," George replied. "We let those scorpion things out of the cave. Ain't you got it yet Jake? Everything that's happened here ain't because of the little people. We did it."

"You didn't know any better," Jake started.

"That ain't no kind of excuse a man should be making, and you know it, little brother," George said softly. "Do I have your promise?"

"You have it... for what it's worth. I ain't getting out of these ropes any time soon. "

"Have faith little brother," George said. "Mother always said the Lord will provide when times are at their darkest."

The Pastor spoke from beside Jake.

"I've been telling him that for weeks, but he ain't listening."

"Is you really a Pastor?" George asked.

"I was, once," the man in black said, almost wistfully. "A long time ago."

"Do you still know the words?" George said plaintively. "I'm in sore need of some words Pastor."

The Pastor nodded.

"You're on a hard path son," he said. "But the Lord is walking beside you every step of the way."

The Pastor started to talk to George. Jake left him to it. What he'd seen done in God's name in the Army had left him with no stomach for bible thumping. Not for himself anyway, although he was glad of the comfort George would take from it.

Jake was surprised to notice he could see George's face clearly.

Daylight came in from outside. It looked soft and diffuse, and Jake soon realized why. Rain pattered on the stone at the entrance to the cave.

Every rainy day after that they fed another of us to the beasts.

A cold shiver ran up Jake's spine that had nothing to do with the damp of the cave.

Chapter 19

Frank came out of a dream of warm sunshine to feel heat on his face. His eyelids were gummed together with sleep. He tried to raise his left hand to rub them clear, but his hand refused to respond to the command. He rolled over slightly, towards the warmth, wiping his eyes on his right forearm. He lay next to the fire that had warmed the right side of his body. The left side felt as cold as a slab of stone.

And damned near as inflexible.

He tried to sit up. It took three attempts, the third taking all the strength he had in his right arm. The left hung uselessly at his side sending drumming pain all through him when he tried to move it. He groaned as he pushed himself upright.

Pat was by his side in seconds. The big man helped him sit up.

"How you feeling, Frank?"

Terrible. I ache all over, my arm feels like it's going to fall off, I'm weak, light headed and I might upchuck at any second.

"Better," he said to Pat, and managed a smile. The big man smiled back. He went to the back of the alcove and came back with the water skins and some hard tack.

"We got us some jerky too," Pat said. "But I figured we better save something. We might be here for a while, what with waiting for you getting better an' all?"

Frank nodded, too weak to speak. He noticed that Pat carried the pistol in his right hand.

"Trouble?" he said, pointing at the gun.

Pat shook his head.

"Nothin'special. The big cat ain't deaded though. I done heard him a-roaring and a-mewling most of the night. And there's some big cows out there somewhere too."

It was only then that Frank noticed it was daylight. He pushed himself to the edge of the cliff and looked out over the valley.

"Any sign of Jake and the others?" he asked.

Pat shook his head.

"Do you think they're okay Frank?"

Frank tried to keep it light.

"They'll be back at the Creek having breakfast and wondering where we're at," he said. "And then they'll come looking for us."

Pat didn't look convinced.

"Do you think?" he said quietly.

Now that Frank was fully awake he saw that Pat's eyes had sunk inwards, black bags underneath showing that the big man was dog-tired.

"Did you stay up all night big man?"

Pat nodded.

"I had to keep watch. Just in case. Ain't gonna let that big cat no-where near you again."

Frank nodded.

"Thanks big man. Now it's my turn. Get my pipe and give me the gun. I'll keep watch for a stretch."

He knew just how tired the big man was when he got no argument back. Pat lay down.

"There's plenty of wood," he said. "Ain't no need to go looking for more. Just keep stoking the fire."

And with that he was asleep.

Frank got the smoke going before scanning the valley.

It was still early morning. A watery sun tried to poke through thin cloud far away to the East. A fine mist hung over the valley floor and rain fell softly all around.

A bellow came from his right.

Pat's big cows?

But these were no cows. The herd came into view through the mist. In the lead was a large bull, tusks bent in a huge arc in front of it, sweeping aside the snow to reach the grass underneath. Frank had seen something close once before, many years ago, at a circus in Augusta. There they had called it a Pachyderm. It had been a sad looking gray thing the size of two horses and as tame as an old dog. What he saw now was no tame beast.

It was hard to judge size from his elevated position, but as far as he could tell the bull stood near ten feet high at the shoulder. It was covered head to tail in thick matted fur that looked black in the dim dawn light. The beast raised a long trunk and bellowed again. Behind him the herd joined in. Thirty or more of them had now appeared from the mist. The noise echoed around the valley as they headed for the lake.

Watering time.

The big bull snorted as it got close to the water, and slowed down. The herd slowed to a stop behind it. The bull used its trunk to sniff the air cautiously. It stomped the ground with a noise that once more echoed around the cliffs. Behind it the herd bellowed.

They look skittish. Like cattle that know a cougar is around.

The bull stood there for some time. It swayed from side to side, stomping the ground again and again. Eventually it moved towards the water.

Either it has decided it is safe... or they are so thirsty, they have to take the risk.

Frank soon saw that it was indeed too risky. Long gray shapes showed in the lake, creeping just under the water.

Scorpions.

He could see them from on high, but the bull, being down at water level, would have no idea of the danger.

The herd moved forward as one, bellowing as they came, suddenly excited.

The ones at the front didn't stand a chance.

The scorpions came out of the water like trout jumping for a fly, latching themselves onto the beasts at trunk, legs and necks. Tails whipped, sending barbs deep into flesh through the hair.

Three of the shaggy brutes staggered, their legs going weak.

The big bull went berserk. The long tusks tossed from side to side. Scorpions flew in the air, some splashing in the lake only to come scuttling back again, others landing on their backs in the slush only to swivel and turn upright in one smooth move.

The bull stomped one of the scorpions into a pulp but two others latched claws onto his trunk. He bellowed in pain and swung the trunk violently from side to side. The scorpions hung on. A barbed tail sunk deep into the beast's shoulder. He buckled, then bellowed his fury. A massive foot squished another scorpion, but the bull was weakening fast. Another barbed tail hit him, just beneath the eye. This time he fell, with a thud that Frank heard even on the cliff above.

The scorpions swarmed over him like ants to sugar.

Three other shaggy beasts had also fallen the same way. Four mounds of the scorpions writhed, claws clacking. The water of the lake flowed red as they stripped meat from bone as effectively as any Augusta butcher could.

Away from the shoreline the remainder of the shaggy herd bellowed mournfully.

But none approached the water.

Some of the scorpions carried chunks of bloody flesh in their claws, some pieces near as big as the scorpions themselves. They soon formed a long straggling line along the near shore of the lake as they headed back to the stream.

Suddenly Frank remembered the small waterfall and the gory remains on the shelf.

They're headed back to the cave. Back to their larder.

They're storing food for their young.

A chill ran down his spine that no amount of stoking the fire would shift.

He lit up another pipe and watched the beasts that were left finish stripping the shaggy bull.

Suddenly a drumbeat started up on the far side of the valley.

The scorpions stopped working on the shaggy beasts. Claws lifted in the air, as if tasting the sound.

The drum beat got louder. It seemed to be coming from the same area where Frank had seen the smoke the day before. The scorpions slid back into the lake and, moving like gray shadows, they headed straight for the source of the noise.

Chapter 20

George's head jerked up when the drumbeat started.

"They'll be coming for me soon," he said. "Remember your promises, Jake. I ain't wanting no fuss. I done made my peace with God and the Pastor here."

Jake could hardly speak.

"I ain't gonna just let you die George. You can't ask me to do that."

George spoke softly.

"Little brother, I'm ready. Better a quick death than rotting in this cave. I want to see the sky and feel the air on my face, just once more afore I go. Let me go."

Jake couldn't think of a single thing to say, but George wasn't finished.

"There's one more thing I done remembered. When we first got here, they fed us better. We had fish, and meat that tasted like coney and deer. But after a week or two that all stopped. You see what that means, don't you?"

Jake couldn't get his brain to focus, but the Squire was paying attention.

"Something is eating the small prey? And stopping these people from getting their share?"

George nodded. He coughed, and more blood ran down his chest. Jake saw with increasing horror that there seemed to be solid lumps of tissue among the blood.

"And we know what that something is. Judging by some of the noises I've been hearing, they've been making a start on bigger beasts. But that ain't the main problem. The main problem is what happens when they finish with chowing down on everything in this valley and move out to Ruby Creek."

Irish Jim saw kelpies in the lake. And we killed one that was going after the horses.

They've already started.

There was a noise at the front of the cave. The drumming got louder, and a soft rustling told them that a group of the small people was approaching.

"George," Jake whispered. "Don't go."

George started to cough again, and fought to speak through bloody lips.

"Remember Jake," he whispered. "No fussing."

Jake sat quietly with tears rolling down his cheeks as the small people, almost reverentially, got George to his feet and herded him out of the alcove. They didn't need to use their spears. George didn't show any signs of putting up a fight.

He looked back just once.

"Remember your promises little brother," he said. "And tell Maureen I thought of her every night."

Then George was gone.

The drumbeat speeded up, and got louder. A soft chanting joined it. It sounded almost like church music, almost peaceful.

But peaceful was the last thing Jake felt. He started to struggle against his bonds.

"George," he shouted. "George!"

He thrashed from side to side until the ropes tore at his skin. But he was tied too tight.

"George!" he shouted again.

"Hush lad," the Pastor said quietly. "Remember your promise."

"Fuck the promise," Jake said, struggling harder against the ropes.

The Pastor spoke softly but his voice had a hard edge to it.

"If I could get out if these bonds I'd smack you on the head until you went quiet. Do you want the last thing he hears to be you breaking your word? You need to be better than that."

Jake slowly calmed as the Pastor's words sank in.

"That's better," the Pastor said. "Now pray with me."

"I done told you, I don't go for no churching."

"But your brother did. So do it for him."

The Pastor started to pray. Jake had been expecting something about the Vale of Death or walking in the Shadow of Evil, but the older man surprised him.

Come let us praise the Lord with joy: let us joyfully sing to God our saviour.

Let us come before his presence with thanksgiving; and make a joyful noise to him with psalms.

For the Lord is a great God, and a great King above all gods.

For in his hand are all the ends of the earth: and the heights of the mountains are his.

The Pastor stopped, but the drumbeats went on. "We are all God's children," he said. "We three here, your brother, and the people who, in their fear, have taken him. All of us are God's children, and he will watch over us."

Somewhere outside George began to scream.

Chapter 21

There are people over there. A lot of them.

Frank guessed it might be a native tribe. Many of the natives had moved north and west ahead of the ever-growing push of settlers, and it was logical that some would end up in the mountains.

The drums got louder, and were soon joined by singing. Frank could no longer see the dark shapes of the scorpions, but he had no doubt they were still moving towards the sound.

The screams, when they came, jolted him to the core.

Is that Jake? Or the Squire?

Frank looked round hastily. Pat still slept, for which Frank was grateful.

That ain't a noise the big man needs to hear.

The screams got louder still, loud enough to overwhelm the drumming and singing. Mercifully they did not last long. They cut off abruptly. The drums and singing also stopped and silence descended on the valley.

In some ways, this is worse. I need to do something.

Frank tried to push his body upright, but he was still as weak as a baby. Lifting the pistol proved almost too much effort for him. He got the gun as far as his lap and nestled it there, cocked and ready should it be needed.

He knew that if those drums started up again he would have to move, but for now rest was all he could do; rest, and try to have enough strength ready for when it was needed.

The fire crackled loudly. He threw two more logs on it. Sometime soon he'd have to wake Pat and send the man off to look for more firewood. But Pat slept the sleep of the just, thumb in his mouth, smile on his face and a snore on his lips.

I'll give him a while longer yet.

Frank turned back to the scene in the valley.

The scorpions below made quick work of the shaggy beasts. Soon there was little left but bone and tattered skin. One by one the scorpions joined the end of the line departing off towards the stream until only the gory remains were left behind.

The remainder of the pachyderm herd set up a mournful bellow. They stood, heads swaying, trunks dragging on the grass, moving to a rhythm that only they understood. But they came no closer to the water. Seconds later they turned and moved off – soon to be lost in the mist and fog.

Then something large and black swooped down from above. At first Frank took it for a crow, then his sense of perspective kicked in. It was the first of many eagles to descend to pick over the bones.

Once more the valley fell deathly quiet, the only sound the crackling of the fire behind him and the steady drip of rainwater onto the rock beyond the overhang.

Well, you wanted solitude Frank. Looks like you've got it.

He smoked another pipe. He was getting through his tobacco fast, but the way things were, he might not be around long enough to get to the bottom of the pouch. His shoulder ached, alternating hot and cold. He'd rolled over onto it while he slept, and the pressure had caused blood to seep through Pat's bandages. He touched the cloth and his fingers came away tacky.

He was also trying not to think of where Pat had got the cloth. It felt suspiciously like the material of an undershirt, and if that was the case, he knew for a fact that Pat hadn't changed it for weeks.

Blood loss now or gangrene later. Smoke them while you've got them.

There was no more movement from the far side of the valley. The figures he'd seen earlier had all gone back into the cave. The only sign of life was the eagles. They worked frantically on the carcasses, tearing away at the scraps of meat the scorpions had left behind.

Suddenly a roar echoed around the valley. The eagles took flight, black wings flapping furiously until they got high enough to glide into a thermal. A long orange body came into view below.

The cat. It's still alive.

It might still be alive, but it was wounded. It limped badly, favoring the leg where Pat had cut into the shoulder. The eagles stayed circling above it, and occasionally swooped down close, trying to scare the beast away from the carcasses. The cat studiously ignored them for the most part, and settled next to the remains of the big bull, tearing and rending the gory mess that was all that was left.

The eagles got more frenzied – and more careless. One made the mistake of swooping too close. The cat showed that, although injured, it was still a predator. Fast as a rattlesnake strike it pulled the eagle out of the air and smacked it hard to the ground. It tore the bird apart swiftly and efficiently.

Above the cat the other birds lost interest. They rose serenely in the thermals and were soon lost from Frank's view. The cat stayed next to the big bull's remains. It lay down with a chunk of meat between its paws. It looked in no hurry to leave.

"I done knew it weren't deaded," Pat said at Frank's side. The big man's eyes were bleary, but he had dragged himself over to sit down and look over the valley.

"Didn't mean to wake you big man," Frank said.

Pat smiled.

"Weren't as if it were any feather bed. I reckon my back has had enough of lying on rock for a while."

Frank motioned down at the cat.

"It's limping bad though," he said. "You hurt it, Pat. It'll think twice before coming at us again."

Pat didn't look convinced.

Frank shifted his buttocks, aware that all the sitting had stiffened his back until he wasn't sure he'd be able to get up again.

"Give me a hand here, Pat," he said. "Help me up."

Pat grabbed him by his good arm and heaved. A second later Frank was standing, but his head still thought he was sitting. A wave of dizziness hit and the world spun around him.

"Thanks," he managed to say. The world slowed and steadied.

Pat handed him the pistol.

"Stay here Frank. I'll get us some more firewood."

"Don't go out of sight Pat," Frank said. "I'll cover you."

The pistol felt like a lump of lead in his hand and he wasn't sure he'd be able to lift it, let along fire it.

But Pat doesn't have to know that.

Pat climbed down off the ledge and started gathering dead wood around the tree line.

Frank looked down to the plain. Eagles were once more tearing at the carcasses.

The big cat was nowhere to be seen.

Chapter 22

Long after the screams stopped, Jake could still hear them, ringing in his head. He knew he would be hearing them for a long time to come.

Probably for the rest of my life.

A wave of despair washed over him, bringing a deep-seated tiredness with it. He recognized the feeling; it had become an old friend back in the penitentiary.

Would have been best to have left me there to rot George. Best for you, best for everybody.

The Pastor and the Squire did not intrude on his grief, and for that he was thankful.

After a while the small people arrived back in the cave. He heard them, sounding happy, cheerful even, as they prepared food. When they brought the thick steaming gruel Jake refused to look in their faces; he had promised George he would try to save them.

But I ain't promised to like them.

Besides, before I can start thinking of saving them, I need to stop them from killing me.

He ate every drop of the gruel though. That was something else he remembered from the penitentiary. Never turn down a meal, as you never know which one will be your last.

He waited until they were alone once more before talking to the other two.

"I'm sorry about your brother," the Squire started, but Jake interrupted him.

"I'll get to mourning when we've got time," he said. "I need to know if either of you have any good ideas. We can't just sit here and let them take us one by one."

"I've been testing the ropes," the Pastor said. "They're as strong as any I've come across. I can't get free, not even a small way."

The Squire smiled.

"I have been working on our escape plan," he said. "I managed to move my saber out of the scabbard. I have a very small piece of cold steel exposed, and have been able to start work on the rope."

Jake looked down. He could see where the Squire's hands were tied at his back. He had indeed started on some rope; pieces were frayed and torn. He still had a long way to go. The effort had already raised numerous cuts on the man's hands. Blood dripped steadily to the cave floor.

The Squire smiled, and for the first time Jake saw strain there.

"I will work on it when I can," the Squire said. "But the pain is severe and I need frequent rests. Bear with me. I'll have you out of here in no time."

The Pastor laughed.

"And then what? Shall we take a quiet stroll along the valley floor? How do you suggest we get back to Ruby's Creek? And even then, we will not be safe."

"The others will come," Jake said softly.

The Pastor laughed again.

"It seems you have learned the benefits of faith lad. As for me, I am finding mine to be sorely tested."

"They will come," Jake said.

But the more he said it, the more it sounded like he was trying to convince no one but himself.

They will come.

Chapter 23

Frank sidled to the cliff edge and looked down, trying to ignore the drips of rainwater that ran down his neck under his jerkin. Pat was ten feet below, collecting wood.

"You want to hurry up there big man?" Frank said, trying to keep things light. "I'm freezing my balls off up here."

"Ain't no whores around to use them on anyways," Pat shouted back, and laughed, as if he'd just made the funniest joke in the world.

Frank wasn't laughing. He scanned the fringes of the forest, watching for any movement.

"Is there anything wrong Frank?" Pat asked. The big man by now had two armfuls of wood. Frank saw, dismayed, that the axe was still up on the ledge. It was leaning against the cave wall near the fire.

"No problem Pat. Just get your arse back up here."

Just as Pat started to clamber, with difficulty, back towards the ledge, the cat walked slowly out of the trees behind him.

Frank tried to keep his voice calm.

"Come on, Pat," he said. "Get a move on."

The big man looked up. He must have seen something in Frank's eye, for he stopped climbing.

"What is it Frank?"

The cat started to creep closer, head and shoulders down close to the ground.

It's stalking him.

"Just fucking move," Frank shouted.

Pat was so shocked he obeyed without thinking. Frank lifted the pistol. His wrists trembled and shook. He got both hands round the grip and sighted along the barrel. It wavered alarmingly.

I'll never hit anything like this.

The cat crept closer. It was staring at Pat with cold intensity and total focus.

"Come on," Frank whispered. "Just a bit closer."

He wasn't even sure if the pistol had enough stopping power. It was barely enough to put a man down without him getting back up again. This beast might shake it off as easily as a bee-sting.

There's only one way to know.

Pat had almost reached the ledge.

Just a little bit closer.

The pistol was starting to feel like an anchor dragging at his arms.

If I don't shoot now, I might not get another chance.

Pat was still looking at Frank and looked close to tears. He didn't seem to notice the pistol.

"I ain't done nothing wrong have I, Frank?"

"Just keep coming, big man," Frank said. "And get behind me."

As Pat squeezed past, the cat turned its attention to Frank. Frank had the high ground up on the edge of the rock, but he'd seen this beast in action and knew just how fast it was.

Now or never.

The cat hunched, ready to pounce. Frank pulled the trigger. The recoil was too much for him and the gun fell away. He heard it clattering on the rock at his feet, but he was too weak to bend for it. He kept his eyes on the cat.

The bullet had hit just below its left eye. The hole wept blood as the beast pawed at it. It mewled pitifully, but showed no signs of falling down dead.

It raised its head and roared then came forward again.

Chapter 24

Jake's head jerked up when the shot rang out.

They've come.

But even here, with the sound muffled in the depths of the cave, he knew that the shot was somewhere in the distance.

But they are here, in the valley.

The three of them listened, straining to hear. There were no more shots.

"How are you doing with that rope, Squire?" Jake asked.

The man's face was white with pain, and a small pool of blood lay beneath his hands.

The Squire gritted his teeth.

"I think I'm almost halfway. But this hair is tougher than an Egyptian whore's cunny. It could take a while yet."

Our friends may not have a while.

Chapter 25

For the second time in as many days Frank saw death come for him.

And this time I'm just about ready for it.

Yet again it wasn't to be. He felt heat pass by his cheek. A blazing firebrand tumbled through the air and landed on the beast… right next to the gaping wound on its shoulder. Fur started to smolder and burn. The beast spun in a circle, snapping at the flame.

Pat strode past Frank, another burning log in one hand, the axe in another. Calmly, with no sign of fear, he walked up to the cat and stuck the flaming wood right at the wound below its eye. Fur and skin sizzled.

The beast roared again, then howled in pain. It turned to run.

Pat swung the axe, twice. The cat fell, hamstrung on both rear legs. Even then it tried to crawl away. Pat walked forward, raised the axe above his head and brought it down fast. He planted the axe in the dead middle of the skull, almost cleaving it in two. He put his foot on the head and had to put his weight into it as he pulled the axe back out. It finally came away with a terrible suck.

Pat turned back and smiled at Frank.

"Well, that weren't so bad now, were it?"

Frank bent, meaning to retrieve the pistol, but the closer to the ground he got, the dizzier he felt. Pat stepped forward and lifted the pistol.

"Let's get you back up next to the fire, Frank," he said. "Looks like you've had enough excitement for a while."

Amen to that big fella.

Frank let Pat half-carry him back up onto the ledge. He sat down, hard, but was grateful that he didn't have to stand any longer.

"It's deaded this time, ain't it?" Pat said, looking down at where the cat's body lay.

"Yeah, it's deaded Pat," Frank said. "You killed it good."

Pat handed him the pistol.

"You better have this though. I ain't no good with one of those."

Frank nodded at the bloody axe in Pat's hand.

"You make up for it with that chopper there though. Good work Pat. You saved my life. Again. I'm never going to be able to repay you."

Pat looked at the ground, suddenly embarrassed.

"Ain't nothing nobody else wouldn't have done in my place."

To save him further embarrassment Frank pretended to check the pistol while Pat stocked the fire. A couple of minutes later the big man brought Frank some jerky and more water.

"It's not much, but it's all we got."

We're going to have to hunt tomorrow. If we wait too long, I'll be too weak.

Pat pointed down at the cat.

"Could we eat it d'ya think?"

Frank laughed then thought about it.

Maybe. If we get desperate enough.

Frank moved over by the fire. He felt bloodless and cold, and no amount of heat would make any difference. He was just about to lie down and try to get some more sleep when Pat whispered from over at the ledge.

"There's something out there Frank. Something watching us."

Frank dragged himself over to the ledge. He took the pistol with him, but he was certain he'd never be able to lift it. Pat hefted the axe.

"Just there in the trees," Pat whispered. "I seed eyes. Lots of eyes."

I see them too.

Several pairs of yellow eyes stared out from the undergrowth, watching the body of the cat. Seconds later the beasts emerged into the clearing.

Five wolves loped out of the trees. Frank had seen many coyote in his life, but nothing prepared him for the sheer size of these. They were each around eight feet long from snout to haunches, with bushy tails hanging behind. Drool dripped from slavering muzzles showing yellowed canines as long as Frank's index finger. Their breath steamed in the cool air.

The lead male raised his snout and sniffed. He looked straight at Frank, then away again at the cat.

I've been dismissed as an irrelevance.

He quickly noticed why the beasts had lost all natural caution. They were starving. Sharp ribs showed, their skin paper thin, blue veins pulsing. Their flanks were so wasted they were almost skeletal. The large male's mane was the only thing that looked healthy, hanging, silver and majestic from painfully bony shoulders.

They wasted no time with Frank and Pat, but headed straight for the cat's body. They ripped and tore at it with a silent ferocity that chilled Frank to the bone; tearing through skin like wet paper and crunching bone beneath their teeth. Soon their snouts and paws dripped with gore. The cat was laid open from chest to groin.

Frank watched as the lead male took the huge heart, devouring it in two gulps. They gutted and flayed the cat. All the larger pieces of meat were efficiently stripped away and carried off into the woods. Less than twenty minutes later three of the males dragged the, now much smaller, carcass into the trees.

All that was left to show of the big cat was a bloody smear on the slushy ground.

Chapter 26

For the rest of the day Jake waited for rescue. But none came, and there were no more shots from out in the valley.

What if the scorpions got them? What then?

His mind flitted, from their predicament, to George, then just as quickly away again. He could not allow himself to think of George's fate. Not yet, for if he did, the fear he had bubbling just below the surface might break out and engulf him.

The Squire kept working at the ropes, but had to stop for longer and longer spells as the pain from the cuts rendered him almost senseless.

"Tell me a story, lads," the Englishman said sometime in the afternoon. "I need something to keep my mind off the damage I am doing to these fine hands. I feel somewhat like Gulliver in Lilliput."

"Who and where?" Jake asked.

The Squire sighed.

"You tell him, Pastor."

The Pastor laughed.

"I'm afraid I don't understand you either."

The Squire managed a laugh of his own.

"Not only am I among heathens, I'm tied up with a pair of illiterate swine."

He launched into a story taller than any he had told previously, about an Irishman and his many adventures on travels in strange lands. The Squire, as always, proved to be a master storyteller, and like all good tales, it transported the men away to a better place, for a while at least. The tale took a long time in the telling, but Jake was still surprised to note that darkness had started to fall while the Squire talked.

"This Gulliver," Jake asked. "He never came to Montana did he?"

The Squire laughed, then grimaced at a fresh burst of pain.

"Not that I know of. Else the tales may well have been stranger yet. Now forgive me sirs, but I must rest before I can do any more. My arms are sore tired and are refusing to do my bidding anymore."

Two minutes later the Squire was asleep. His snores echoed loudly through the cave.

The Pastor seemed in no mood for talk, so Jake let the encroaching darkness fill him and soon he too fell into a fitful sleep.

Chapter 27

Frank woke slowly. He hadn't even been aware of being asleep. He was sitting upright on the ledge, staring out over the valley.

Dusk had fallen. The lake sat quiet under a thin film of whispy mist. Behind him Pat lay snoring gently by the fire. Frank forced his aching limbs into movement to throw more logs on the flames.

I'm supposed to be on watch!

After the wolves disappeared Pat had wanted to stand watch, but Frank insisted that the big man get some rest. Frank had sat, smoking another pipe and watching the valley. The only activity had been the soaring of eagles above the carcasses near the lake, and soon even they moved on as the mist came down and blanketed everything in soft gray. With no other stimulus to occupy his mind, Frank had slipped, unnoticed into sleep.

I can't allow it to happen again.

His shoulder had gone stiff as stone, but the ache was less that it had been. He also felt stronger. He wasn't going to be using his left arm for a while, but he was beginning to think he could manage to walk without throwing up.

In the morning, we'll go and look for Jake and the others. I just hope we're not too late.

They'd barely had time for contemplation since entering the valley, but Frank was well aware that they had heard no shooting but their own since they had first faced the big cat. That was more than twenty four hours ago.

If they are still here, we should have heard something by now.

He pushed the thought away.

His first priority was Pat, and after that, finding the others. Tomorrow, they would go down into the valley, a bit more carefully now they knew some of the dangers that waited.

And if we don't find Jake and the others in an hour or so, I'll head back to the creek.

In the back of his mind he kept seeing the glistening scorpion eggs on the walls of the newly opened cavern. He knew he'd have to deal with that, sometime.

Let's not get too far ahead of ourselves here. One thing at a time.

The next time he stoked the fire Pat woke up.

"Take a spell yourself Frank," Pat said as he stood. "I ain't going back to sleep anytime soon, and, pardon my French, but you look like shit."

So much for feeling better.

But Frank didn't argue. He lay down by the fire. He made sure the pistol was near his hand, put his head on his shoulder bag, and was asleep in seconds.

He was too tired to dream.

Some time later he came up out of sleep to feel hot breath at his cheek. At first he thought he must have rolled over too near the fire again. Then he heard the breathing, hot and heavy.

It smelled of raw meat.

He opened his eyes and looked up at the yellow stare and drooling muzzle of the large wolf. It stood over him, sniffing at the wound on his shoulder.

It has smelled the blood.

Out of the side of his eye he saw that the fire had gone out.

Where's Pat?

Slowly, so as not to panic the beast, he inched his hand towards the pistol. The wolf started to paw at the bandages on his shoulder. The pain went up a notch, then flared in a searing heat as the wound split and began to bleed again.

The wolf lowered its head and started to lick roughly at the blood oozing through the bandage.

Frank got his hand on the butt of the pistol.

Is it loaded?

He couldn't remember, but it didn't matter. Either it was loaded, in which case he had a chance, or the wolf was about to make a meal out of his arm.

The wolf's drool dripped in ropy strands and he had to twist his face aside to avoid getting it in his mouth. The animal growled from deep in its throat. It opened its jaws and lunged...just as Frank brought the pistol up and put a shot in its left ear from right up close.

The noise rang in his head as he pushed the wolf off and rolled away. Pat woke up and yelled loudly in fright. Another beast left the cave fast. Frank only saw its tail as it fled.

Frank raised the pistol again and pointed it at the wolf. It didn't move. When he stood over it he saw why. Although there was only a small powder burn at the left ear, the whole right hand side of its head was blown out; brain and bone scattered against the cave wall.

Pat came over and looked down at the body.

"Can we eat this one Frank? Can we?"

Chapter 28

The Pastor woke Jake in the morning.

"Jake!" he said, insistently. "Jake!"

Jake's first thought was that he'd missed breakfast, and that George would need some help out in the fields. Then he remembered where he was, and the despair hit him like a hammer.

"I done heard you Pastor," he replied. "Ain't no need to shout."

"It is raining again," the Pastor said softly.

"Well ain't that a good reason to wake me up," Jake said. "I was having a fine dream about pancakes and maple syrup."

"Save some for me," the Squire said behind him. "And a pot of Rosy-Lee would go down a treat."

The Pastor looked at both of them as if they were mad.

"It never does any good to make light of a situation," he said.

The Squire laughed.

"In my experience, it never does any good not to."

"I thought I heard a shot in the night," the Pastor went on. "I was only half-awake, and it only came once. But it was another shot, I'm sure of it."

"Then chin up, old man," the Squire said. "Today we'll have our freedom once more."

The Pastor looked glum.

"I have a shadow on my soul this morning," he said. "A chill that no amount of praying will shift. I hope you are right. But I fear you are wrong."

The Squire was already back working on his bonds. More blood dripped steadily from his wrists and his hands looked pale and swollen like ripe fruit. But still he smiled.

"Bear up, Pastor. I am almost there. Another hour and we'll be out

99

in the sunshine. That will lift your chill soon enough."

They were not given the hour.

A rustling came from the main cave. The little people thronged at the entrance of the alcove seconds later, all of them carrying the short stone spears, holding them out in front of their bodies as if expecting an attack.

"I would try to use charm on them," the Squire said laughing. "But I'm having a hard time distinguishing which are the women-folk."

The small people came forward warily.

The Pastor looked straight at them, and spoke, his voice resonating and booming.

Comfort those who sit in darkness, mourning 'neath their sorrow's load. For the glory of the Lord now o'er earth is shed abroad; and all flesh shall see the token that His word is never broken.

"Amen Pastor," the Squire said softly.

After much high chattering the small people started to poke and prod at the Pastor, urging him to his feet.

"Take me," the Squire shouted. "Take me."

But the small people had made their choice. They seemed excited, eager almost as they poked their spears into the Pastor's ribs. The man in black continued to stare at them as they began to push him up from the floor of the cave.

"It seems it is my turn to stand up and be counted," he said.

Jake thrashed and cursed, but his bonds held tight.

"Quiet lad," the Pastor said as he stood upright. "You made your brother a promise. Now make me the same one. You will save these children."

Jake spat.

"These are no children," he said. "They will stand by and watch you get fed to yon scorpions, then come back here and laugh about it."

"Nevertheless, you will save them," the man in black said as they led him away. He shouted back, having to raise his voice to be heard. "The only way to save yourself is to save them."

"What the hell does that mean," Jake shouted, but the Pastor had already been led off out of the cave.

"Work faster," Jake said at the Squire. "We've got to get out of here."

The Englishman's face was white with pain and blood ran freely to pool on the floor beneath his hands.

"Righty-ho, Gaffer," he said, and tried to smile. "I'll be right with you."

Outside, the drums started to beat.

Chapter 29

Frank heard the drums start as they skirted the carcasses of the shaggy beasts.

For the first time since the original cat attack he felt almost human.

Last night Pat had butchered the wolf like an expert and then slow cooked it in stages over the fire.

"You done this before big man?" Frank had asked.

"Only with jackrabbits," Pat replied. "But a wolf ain't much more than a big jackrabbit with teeth anyhow."

It took some time for Pat to prepare and cook the wolf. Frank slipped in and out of a fitful sleep while Pat turned the makeshift spit. At some point later Pat announced it was ready.

"Well, as ready as it's every gonna be."

It had been surprisingly easy to eat. The meat seemed to give Frank renewed strength and vigor. They had taken turns on watch through the remainder of the night but there were no more visits by the pack. Just before dawn Frank heard their high ethereal howling in the hills away to the west, and guessed a new pack leader was being chosen. The howls went on for many minutes, hanging, almost tangible, over the otherwise silent valley. The cloud cover had lifted and the stars sparkled like diamonds in the crisp night air.

A man could get to like this place... if he could just live long enough to enjoy it.

Frank had a smoke as the sun came up, then he woke Pat.

"Come on big man. Let's go and find our friends."

"You feeling well enough Frank?" Pat asked.

Frank had nodded.

Better than them at any rate I suspect.

They got as much of the remaining meat as they could carry into Pat's back-pack and tossed the rest of the remains into the trees. Frank loaded the pistol and slung the holster at his waist... his shoulder wouldn't take the pressure.

Big Pat had refused to let go of the large axe.

"I'll hold onto this," he said. "Just in case there's any more surprises."

Ten yards inside the trees they found what was left of the big cat; a small, almost neat, pile of skin and bone with only scraps of flesh left on either. Wolf tracks led away north and upwards. Frank led Pat down towards the valley floor.

They had headed down the hill just as a rain shower swept through the valley. Within a minute they were soaked through most of the layers of their clothing and the ground underfoot got treacherous and slushy..

Next time I want to find solitude, I think I'll try California.

As the terrain levelled out near the foot of the slope the going got easier, but Frank got steadily weaker.

"I knew there was a reason to bring that chopper Pat. Do me a favor and cut me a walking stick?"

He lit a smoke and kept his eyes on the trees while Pat searched for an appropriate sapling. There had been no sound since they left the ledge, but that meant nothing. Wolves could move as silent as shadows, even ones as big as these.

"Keep in sight Pat," he shouted

The big man cut Frank a sapling that was near six feet tall and almost as thick as Frank's wrist. He leaned his weight on it and it didn't crack or bend.

And it'll also come in handy as a club... if I have the strength to wield it.

After that walking got easier.

But I can't go far.

Hopefully, just far enough.

When they reached the valley floor Pat's eyes went wide. Frank saw he was looking at the carcasses strewn on the lakeshore.

"What were these Frank? Big cows?"

He was about to move closer when Frank pulled him back.

"Yeah. Big cows. And near as daft as you big man. Stay as far from the water as you can," he said. "And if you see any of those scorpion things, holler and start running."

"There's beasties here?" Pat said, raising the axe.

Frank had been about to agree when the drums started up. It was the same beat he had heard yesterday.

First the drums, then the screaming.

Frank started walking faster, giving the carcasses a wide berth.

"What's them drums for Frank?" Pat asked. Frank had a good idea, but wasn't about to tell the big man.

"I think Jake, or one of the others, is in trouble. Come on Pat, let's hurry."

The drums got louder as they rounded the top end of the lake. About a mile away they saw figures emerge from a cave mouth. There were many small figures, and one larger one, dressed all in black and immediately recognizable, even at a distance.

"Pastor!" Pat shouted, and broke into a run.

Frank struggled along behind, but Pat got further ahead with every step.

They were still several hundred yards short when the Pastor started to sing, his voice carrying high and clear above the drums.

Then let our songs abound, and every tear be dry,

We're marching through Immanuel's ground, to fairer worlds on high.

Out on the lake the water started to surge and boil, as if many creatures struggled to make their way to shore. Several tall tails breached the surface, barbed tips twitching.

We're not going to make it in time.

Pat was nearly fifty yards ahead now. Frank saw the small people tie the Pastor to four posts on the ground near the shore.

"Leave him be," Pat screamed, and ran faster, getting even further ahead of Frank.

Frank fired a shot into the air, hoping to get the attention of the little people long enough to distract them, but there was no response. They finished tying up the Pastor and stood back as scorpions started to emerge from the water.

The Pastor could obviously see them, but he kept singing, his voice never faltering, even as twenty scorpions broke onto the shore. They came forward slowly, claws raised in the air setting up a cacophony of clacking.

The little people started to sing, their chant counter-pointing that of the Pastor. They were so intent on watching the scorpions they did not see Pat rush up behind them.

104

"Pastor!" the big man shouted. He had almost reached the back of the group of small people.

He was ten yards too late as the first scorpion clamped a claw on the Pastor's left leg and snipped.

Chapter 30

Jake heard the shot.

They're closer. Much closer.

The Pastor's singing echoed around them, even deep in the cave.

We're marching to Zion, beautiful, beautiful Zion.

We're marching upward to Zion, the beautiful city of God.

The sound of clacking echoed alongside.

"Hurry!" Jake shouted to the Squire.

"Whatever you say, Gaffer," the Squire responded.

He pushed down, hard, with his hands. Blood spurted in a fountain, spraying the cave wall. But the Squire was free. He shuffled over to Jake, pulling out the saber. More blood gushed down the blade where it cut through Jake's bonds.

"Get going man," the Squire whispered, whipping of his belt and starting to set a tourniquet on his left arm. "I'll be right behind you. This is just a scratch."

Jake left the alcove at a run.

He found their weapons just at the entrance to the main cave. He lifted the Pastor's pistol belt and bandoleer and, peering against the sudden glare, headed for the lake. He was just in time to see blood spray in the air as the scorpion snipped off the Pastor's lower leg.

"Pastor!"

Jake saw Big Pat run into the crowd of small people, scattering them like skittles. The big man leapt over the Pastor's body and began hacking at the leading scorpion, trying to keep its claws from doing any more damage to the Pastor.

Remarkably, the Pastor was still singing, even as blood sprayed from the stump.

A scorpion's tail rose high in the air over Pat's head. The big man was too intent on chopping at the first to notice. Jake tried not to hurry

106

as he stopped and raised the pistol. His first shot missed, but the second blew the barbed tip apart. The tail came down and the stump hit Pat harmlessly on the shoulder.

Another shot rang in Jake's ears. Frank Collins staggered up to stand beside him. The man looked gray; eyes sunk deep into their sockets. Blood seeped at his left shoulder, but the pistol in his right hand was held steady and firm.

At the sound of the shots the small people scattered.

"Pat," Jake shouted. "Get the Pastor and get out of there. We'll cover you."

More of the Scorpions, drawn by the noise and the blood, tried to crowd around the Pastor. Pat was pressed hard to keep them at bay, and although Jake and Frank shot round after round into them it barely slowed them.

The Pastor still sang, but his voice was noticeably weaker, barely audible above the excited clacking of the mandibles.

"We've got to get away from the water," Frank shouted as he reloaded his pistol. "They don't move far from the water."

"Pat," Jake shouted. "I done told you. Get the hell outa there."

"I ain't goin' nowhere without the Pastor," Pat replied. He swung the axe and split a scorpion from head to tail. The acrid smell tickled Jake's nostrils even at this distance.

Jake and Frank moved closer and put shots in the creatures closest to the big man, buying him enough time to chop away the ropes covering the Pastor. They kept up the covering fire as Pat began to drag the man away from the scorpions. As if sensing that their prey would elude them they surged forward.

"Pat!" Jake shouted. A scorpion loomed over him, claws wide, ready to snip.

A rapid volley of rifle fire from behind them blew the front of its head into fragments of shell and gore. The Squire ran towards them, laying down more fire.

The armed men shot bullet after bullet into the advancing scorpions. The stink of burnt powder and scorpion gore assaulted Jake's nostrils. Pat had one hand dragging the Pastor, the other trying to hold off the scorpions with the axe.

Jake ran out of ammo, just as a claw reached for him. He dodged to one side and drew his saber. He slashed at the claw. The shock ran up his arm as if he'd hit stone. The claw clacked right in front of his face.

He fended it off with the saber. The sword slid down the serrated edge of the mandible and lodged in the big joint at the elbow. The scorpion pulled back suddenly, as if in pain.

They have a weak spot.

Jake targeted his swings after that, chopping at the joints of any beast that came close. Soon he had a small pile of claws at his feet while beasts scuttled around waving oozing stumps in the air. A barbed tail swung towards him, but the Squire had been watching Jake. The Englishman had his own saber drawn. He cleaved the tail in two with one stroke.

Pat reached the defenders, still dragging the Pastor behind him.

"Pat," Frank said softly. "You can let go. He's gone."

Jake looked down.

The Pastor stared up at him from dead eyes.

"I ain't leaving him here for those things to eat him," Pat shouted through tears. "I just ain't."

Jake patted the big man's shoulder.

"Nobody's getting left," he said. "Get him away Pat. We'll cover you."

They backed away slowly allowing Pat to drag the Pastor's body off. They got nearly fifty yards from the lake before they realized the scorpions were no longer following. The beasts clacked their claws in the air, but came no further.

They almost sound disappointed.

As one the scorpions turned and, in a scuttling run, headed back to the water.

Jake almost allowed himself to breathe... just as the first stone spear flew from the cave mouth and landed at his feet.

Jake looked around. The Pastor was dead, Pat had a gash on his right arm that he hadn't noticed but was leaking blood, the Squire looked as white as a sheet, and Frank Collins was about ready to keel over.

Doing a fine job of looking after everybody here Jake. A damned fine job.

Another spear thudded into the ground a foot from Jake's right foot.

"We need to retire and regroup, Gaffer," the Squire said weakly.

Jake nodded.

"But where can we go that is safe?"

Pat's head came up. He almost smiled.

"We know a good place, don't we, Frank? We can get a fire going and be safe and warm in no time. Can't we Frank? Can't we?"

Frank nodded. He looked too weak to speak.

Pat hefted the Pastor's body over his shoulder as if he was little more than a bag of flour.

Two more spears landed nearby. That decided the matter for Jake.

"Lead the way big man," Jake said. "You're the boss."

Chapter 31

By the time they made it back to the rock ledge Frank was dead on his feet. Fresh blood leaked through the bandages at his shoulder. His wounds throbbed hotly in time with his heart. He leant heavily on the walking stick all the way up the hill and had to be helped bodily up the short clamber to the overhang.

Once there he sat on the ledge beside the Squire while Pat and Jake buried the Pastor. It looked to be hard going for them, as the ground was rocky and partially frozen and they only had the axe as a tool. But Pat worked at it like a man possessed and only rested when Jake insisted on taking his turn.

The Squire and Frank shared several pipes from the Squire's supply while the Englishman calmly cauterized the slice wounds in his hands and wrists. Several times he winced in pain, but still he smiled when Frank passed him a chunk of meat.

"Meat thickens the blood," Frank said. "At least that's what Pat kept telling me last night."

"I've heard it said," the Squire replied. He turned the meat over in his hand before taking a bite. "Wolf eh? I ate a jackal once. In Ethiopia. I remember…"

Off he went on another tale, one that helped pass the time until Jake and Pat stood up from the grave. Frank and the Squire helped each other down. They stood around the grave, heads lowered.

After hearing that all the men from the settlement were dead, killed by the scorpions, Pat had gone quiet and still. He insisted on wearing the Pastor's clothes. They were a tight fit. Where the cassock had hung loosely on the Pastor it was snug against Pat's broad chest, and he was never going to be able to fasten the duster at the front. But he insisted that he would wear them. Why, Frank had no idea but guessed it might have to do with some churching Pat might have had as a lad. Whatever the reason, he cut an imposing figure in the cassock and black duster.

Somehow it made the big man look intimidating.

The valley is doing something to Pat. Making him into something.

Pat led them into the Lord's Prayer, then the big man sang Abide With Me in a high tenor which seemed to send the whole valley into hushed reverence. They left the Pastor's big bible on the packed earth of the grave. Afterwards Pat stood there for a long time, tears streaming down his cheeks.

Frank and the Squire went back to rest next to the fire, keeping it stoked.

Jake came to join them.

"Well ain't this a fine day," he said wearily, and sat down beside them.

The Squire laughed.

"What we need is a plan of action Gaffer. Something on which to focus our minds."

Jake laughed in reply.

"What I need is some whiskey. But I don't fancy our chances of getting back to Ruby Creek alive."

They sat watching the valley and brought each other up to date on their stories.

"Eggs? There were eggs?" Jake said.

"Thousands of them," Frank replied. "Might even be hatched by now."

Then Jake whistled when Frank told him about the big cat.

"Sounds like the big man has been holding us all together."

Frank looked over to where Pat still stood over the grave.

"I wouldn't be alive without him. From now on, where he goes, I go."

"And there's the question," Jake said. "Where do we go? God knows how many of them scorpions there are between us and safety."

At first Frank had no answer. He stared down at the valley floor.

He heard them before he saw them, the same deep bellowing from the day before. The herd of shaggy beasts lumbered into view. They stayed well back from the water.

And just as well.

Out on the lake black shapes seemed to glide, just below water level, grouping just off-shore.

They are waiting for the beasts.

The shaggy beasts stamped and bellowed. They tore at the turf with their tusks and threw grass high in the air all around them.

The scorpions lay still, quiet, waiting.

The noise of the bellowing resounded like thunder through the valley.

Still the scorpions didn't move.

Jake looked down, following Frank's gaze.

"It's a standoff," Frank said. "The beasts need water, but can't get any closer, and the scorpions need meat for their young, but I'm guessing they can't get too far out of the water... not in daylight anyways."

"What do you mean, 'need meat for their young'?"

Frank told Jake about the line of scorpions carrying meat back to the cave, and what he thought it meant.

Jake's face broke into a grin.

"You've given me an idea. But rest-up a bit. I need to chew on it a while."

After a while the shaggy beasts gave up and retreated out of sight back up the valley. Slowly the gray shapes under the water drifted off to other parts of the lake, leaving the white bones of the carcasses as the only evidence they'd ever been there.

Chapter 32

Jake left Frank and the Squire sitting on the ledge and went to sit at the fire. After a while Pat came and sat beside him.

"Are you okay Pat?" Jake asked.

The big man was quiet for a long time. Sitting there in the Pastor's cassock and duster he looked like a monk deep in prayer. When he looked up at Jake his eyes were red and rheumy.

"They's all dead Jake," he whispered. "George, Jim, Farting Bill. Everybody. They's all dead."

Jake looked down into the fire.

"I know," he said softly. "But we're still here. The best thing we can do is remember them."

Pat started into the fire for a while longer.

"I aim to do better than that," he said after a time. "I aim to make sure they ain't dead for nothing."

"How are you planning on doing that big man?"

But Pat was in no mood for talking. They sat in silence. Eventually the Squire came and sat with them.

"Frank said you had an idea?" he said to Jake. "A campaign plan?"

Jake nodded.

"I've been thinking. If them scorpions are so keen on taking meat up to the cave, then maybe we need to make sure they get plenty of it. That way, we can slip past them real sneaky-like, while they're occupied, and get back to the Creek."

"Good thinking, Gaffer," the Squire said. "The sooner we get out of this place the better."

"And then what Jake?" Pat said quietly.

Jake smiled.

"Then we pick up George's gold and high-tail it back to somewhere we can spend it."

"No," Pat said.

Just that one word, but it was the first time that Jake could remember Pat disagreeing with him.

"Have you got a better plan big man?"

Pat was quiet for so long that Jake didn't think he was going to answer. And when he did, he stunned Jake into a shocked silence.

"The way I see it, we brought the beasties here," he said. "We started all this death... brought it on ourselves. If we hadn't been so greedy for the damned mother lode, all of this ain't never needed to happen. We gotta fix it Jake. For George's sake. For the Pastor's sake. For the sake of all our friends, and of everything in this valley, and outside. We ain't gonna let more of them scorpion things out into our world. We can't."

That was the longest speech Jake had ever heard from the Irishman, and the most heartfelt. It also echoed in Jake's conscience alongside the promises he'd made back in the cave; to George, to the Pastor... and to myself.

"Okay Pat. Let's hear it."

"I've been thinking," he started.

"Be careful you don't strain anything," the Squire said, then went quiet when he saw the look on Pat's face.

"I've been thinking about Ruby Creek. Well, not about the Creek, but about what we left in the cabins. We've got a lot of black powder Jake. A whole lot."

Jake smiled.

"And if we get all them scorpions down into the cave? Have we enough to send them all to Hell?"

"Well, we surely got enough to stop them climbing back out of it," Pat said. "But first we gotta get them there."

"Leave that to me big man," Jake said. "You ain't the only one who's been thinking."

Chapter 33

Frank heard the conversation from his spot at the ledge, but was too tired to take any part in it.

But I was right. The valley has changed Pat. Whether it's for the better or not only time will tell.

The Squire had left his tobacco pouch, and Frank helped himself to another pipe.

Across the valley floor smoke once more rose from the cave mouth. But there was no more drumming.

I don't think I could take any more drumming.

Images of the fight against the scorpions kept flitting in and out of his mind, and the smell of powder still stung in his nostrils. His hands shook as he lifted the pipe to his lips, and not all of that was due to his tiredness.

The shoulder wound seemed to have stopped seeping for the moment. The Squire had taken a long look at it earlier.

"You should live, man," the Englishman said. "But you won't enjoy it for a while."

The valley lay quiet beneath him. Twice now he had seen an eagle dip towards the lake, only for a scorpion claw to try to snatch the bird from the air. Both times the eagle had escaped; the second in a flurry of feathers.

I was right. Everything in this valley is starving from lack of food or water. The scorpions are killing everything.

Jake came and sat beside him.

"How's the shoulder?"

Frank laughed grimly.

"The arm is still attached. But if you offered me that axe and promised an end to the pain I might take you up on it."

"When we get back to the Creek, there's a case of hard liquor that'll take the edge off that."

Frank laughed again.

"It might as well be on the moon."

Now it was Jake's turn to laugh.

"If you can survive until tomorrow, I'll help you drink it."

"What happens tomorrow?"

Down in the valley the shaggy beasts started to low. Jake smiled.

"Tell me, Frank. Have you ever seen a stampede?"

Chapter 34

Jake gave them the whole of that day and night to rest. He shared most of the watches with Pat while Frank and the Squire rested and recovered as well as they could from their wounds.

Jake spent some time taking inventory of the weaponry. He had the Pastor's pistols. That made four handguns in total between them. The Squire also had a rifle, they had the two sabers, and Pat had his axe. They had sixty cartridges for the pistols and forty for the rifle.

Ain't much to take on a small army of beasts. But it will be enough. It will have to be enough.

He too noticed the change in Pat. The big man spent the time when not on watch just sitting, staring into the fire. He seemed to have soaked up some of the Pastor's quiet stoicism through the cassock. He was calmer somehow.

And maybe smarter.

In the depths of the night, when the other three were asleep and the fire was well stoked, Jake finally allowed himself to think about George.

Pat put me to shame big brother. I was ready to run. Take the gold and find a warm whore. But the big man is on the side of the Lord now, and I guess I'll be doing his bidding. I'll keep my promise to you George. Or die trying.

They ate the last of the wolf for breakfast, helping it down with hard tack and water while Jake laid down his plan.

"A stampede?" the Squire said. "That's your plan? You can't control a stampede of cows. How are we going to control beasts such as those pachyderm? I've seen their like in India. They are docile creatures, hard to rile."

Frank laughed.

"Not these ones. Trust me, we'll get them riled up in no time."

Jake nodded.

"Ain't no beast that can't be riled. Get them in a group, and they can be riled real fast."

The Squire still did not look convinced as they left the rock ledge and made their way down into the valley once more.

"How do we get them to go where we want them to go?" he asked.

Jake smiled. He patted the pistols slung at his hips.

"I've found these to be persuasive in the past. And that rifle of yours is noisy enough to wake the dead themselves." He looked over to where Frank and Pat walked slowly and silently down the trail. Pat had the axe slung over his shoulder. "And if that fails, we'll just set the big man on them. I don't know about you, but he's starting to scare the bejeesus out of me."

The Squire smiled.

"I look at Pat, and think the Pastor himself is still around, watching over us. A good shepherd watching over his flock."

"Let us hope the shepherd can actually do some herding," Jake said as they came out onto the level plain.

All was quiet down by the lakeside, but up the valley to the west Jake could see the lumbering figures of the herd. They seemed to be grazing, moving slowly in a long line, from one side of the valley to the other.

The men walked westward, taking their time, being careful not to spook the beasts.

As they got closer to the herd the men slowed down further, but the animals were too busy eating to pay them any notice. Jake tallied their number and stopped counting at fifty. There were at least ten bull males, with the rest a mixture of females and adolescents. There were no small young. They looked placid, almost like a corralled herd of cows.

"What now, Gaffer?" the Squire whispered.

Jake sent Pat and Frank in a wide circle round the back of the beasts while he and the Squire stood between the herd and any escape to the south. The cliffs bounded the north side, leaving the only route for the beasts to be to the east… towards the lake.

"Ready," Jake said.

"As I will ever be. I'd just like to say, this is the daftest plan since Bonaparte fancied Christmas in Moscow."

Jake waved to Frank, who raised his pistol and fired a round into the air.

Things started to go out of control seconds later.

The beasts took fright immediately, turned away from the noise and lumbered, slowly at first, towards Jake and the Squire. The Squire fired into the air and the beasts stopped as one.

The largest male raised its trunk in the air and bellowed turning in the same movement and heading, not east, but back towards Pat and Frank.

Chapter 35

The rest of the herd turned to follow the large male. They started to pick up speed as they came. Frank saw their death coming for them; several tons of it, on the hoof and coming fast.

He shot in the air again. When that had no effect he fired straight at the lead male. He saw a hole appear in the beast's face just below the left eye, but it didn't slow. It trumpeted loudly in rage. The noise of the herd's feet on the ground rolled like distant thunder.

We're dead.

But Pat had other ideas. He opened the duster coat and held it out on either side like large black wings, flapping, like one of the eagles.

Then he started to run. Not away, but towards the big male.

He let out a roar that was as loud as anything made by the beasts. He flapped the tails of the coat as he went, like a giant bird trying to take off.

On Pat's second roar the large male stopped, too quickly. Three other males ran into it and almost knocked it over. For several seconds the herd was in complete turmoil and the valley was filled with the sound of bellows and trumpets.

Finally the male got its footing. It turned towards the south, but Frank saw that Jake and the Squire had been waiting for that. Jake fired two shots in the air and he too ran towards the herd.

The big male finally turned eastward, gathering speed. The rest of the herd followed suit. Soon the four men ran behind, roaring and hollering, as the beasts thundered towards the lake.

The scorpions were already there, waiting.

The carnage started almost immediately.

The large male had too much momentum. He hurtled headlong through a line of scorpions, trampling and squashing some underfoot at the shore before stumbling into the water. Six scorpions scuttled over him in less than a second. He rose, twice, trying to shake them off, but the thud of their stings sinking into flesh could be heard even at a distance. More of the herd stumbled at the water's edge, trampling on the scorpions, running into each other in a vain attempt to escape. Scorpions came out of the water in wave after wave, ranging in size from four to nine feet long.

There are scores of them. Hundreds.

Claws clacked and chopped at legs and trunks. Blood sprayed high in the air and the trumpeting took on a panicked frenzied note that was terrible to hear. A dozen of the shaggy beasts were down in the water already, little more than heaving mounds of scorpions slicing and dicing through flesh. More were dying by the second as the weight of those at the rear kept pushing the others towards the massed ranks of scorpions. The air was heavy with the tang of coppery blood. There were five or more scorpions for every one of the beasts and soon thirty or more pachyderm lay dead and dying in the water.

The remainder of the herd tried to back away from the shore.

"Keep driving them, lads," Jake shouted, firing his pistol. "It's our only hope."

Pat ran forward again, duster coat flapping. Frank put two shots into the last remaining live male. The herd turned and headed for the water once more.

Within five minutes there were none of them left alive. The four men stood fifty yards back and watched the butchery unfold.

Chapter 36

Several minutes later Jake saw the first scorpion crawl out of the lake carrying a slab of meat. A long line of them developed, stretching away towards the stream at the east-end of the lake.

Well, that went better than I expected.

Pat had tears streaming down his face as he watched the beasts being flayed and chopped. But he stood and watched, and did not avert his eyes.

The old Pat would have his back turned and his eyes closed.

"Well, Gaffer," the Squire said. "What now?"

"Now we wait a while. Ain't no use getting too far ahead of ourselves. Once enough of those beasts have headed back to the cave, we'll follow them."

"And then we kill them," Pat said softly. "Kill them all."

"That's the plan big man."

"Good," Pat said. His eyes were hard as flints.

The mass of scorpions made quick work of their prey. The lake was red as far as the eye could see. Patches of fur and fat floated in a scum on the surface. One by one the scorpions carried meat aloft in their claws, some of the pieces nearly as large as the scorpions themselves.

In the time it took the Squire to smoke a pipe the shaggy beasts were stripped bare. The line of scorpions stretched far into the distance, and only two or three stragglers still chopped and tore at the carcasses. Overhead, eagles gathered in a high spiral.

"Time we were going, lads," Jake said.

The four of them walked towards the line of scorpions, warily at first, then with more confidence as the beasts ignored them, intent on carrying their catch back to the cave.

"It looks like your plan is working, Gaffer," the Squire said.

"Let's hope the rest of it goes as smoothly," Jake replied, but he had half his attention on Pat and Frank. Neither of the two of them had spoken more than a few words all day. Both seemed lost in their thoughts, distant and distracted.

I can understand it with Collins. That shoulder must hurt like the devil. But I can't fathom what's up with the big man. He's changed.

And I ain't sure it's for the better.

They walked alongside a particularly large specimen of the scorpions. It carried a meaty rack of ribs aloft above it, using the large tail to balance the weight. It seemed oblivious to their existence.

Let's hope it stays that way.

The smell, both from the scorpions and the butchered meat, was almost overwhelming. By the time they reached the stream Jake had his mouth covered with a hand, and had to force the gorge down to stop him gagging.

The climb up the hill proved difficult. Pat ended up almost carrying Frank, and the Squire left blood dripping in the snow from reopened wounds in his wrists. By the time they reached the high outcrop where they first entered the valley they were all exhausted. Frank Collins looked like he was near to collapse; white as a sheet, with new blood seeping through the bandages at the shoulder.

They sat on the rim looking out over the valley, trying to catch their breath. Scorpions walked past then, less than ten yards away, but paying them no notice.

"Pat," Jake said. "Stay here and look after Frank. The Squire and I will fetch the powder. Meet us at the mouth of yon cave in an hour."

Pat looked Jake in the eye.

"You ain't gonna run out on us, are you, Jake?"

Such a thought would never even have occurred to the old Pat.

Jake stared back.

"I done promised George, and I done promised the Pastor. Now I'll promise you big man. I ain't going nowhere until we sort this mess out."

Jake rose, groaning at pains in muscles he didn't even know he had.

"Come on Squire. Let's see how quickly we can get down to the Creek and back."

The oil lamps lay in the mud at the lip of the cave. They'd been overturned, and half trampled into the clay. They picked up two. Both still worked when the Squire lit them up.

Jake watched the scorpions going down the passageway. There was just enough room between them for the men to slip in and walk between them. They would have to keep up a good pace to avoid being walked over.

"Are you up to running, Squire?"

"If it means getting out of this valley, I'm up for anything old chap. Lead on, and don't spare the horses."

Jake waited until the next scorpion went down the shaft, then slid quickly into position. The Squire jumped in alongside and together they went down into the dark, hemmed in front and back by two large scorpions.

Chapter 37

The last scorpion went down the hole five minutes after Jake and the Squire. Frank would have been happy to sit on the ledge and watch the valley until Jake came back, but Pat had other ideas.

"What if those beasts ain't had enough food yet Frank?" he asked, looking back down the pit. "What if they decide to come back out? No amount of powder's gonna do any good then."

Frank used up the last of his tobacco and lit up a pipe.

"What do you suggest, Pastor?" he asked, before he realized what he'd said.

"Pastor," Pat said, and smiled. "I think I like that. I think that's what I'll be."

I don't think you just get to choose like that.

He didn't tell Pat what he was thinking. The big man wasn't listening anyway. He still stared down the pit.

"We gotta stop them getting back up here," he said.

Frank laughed bitterly.

"What do you suggest we use Pat? Harsh language?"

The big man rose and hefted the axe.

"If they is all down in the side tunnel, then all we have to do is stop them getting out of there. Between the two of us, we can do that. It ain't hardly wide enough to let one of them out at a time."

"Ain't no need for that. Jake will be back soon with the powder," Frank said, and was dismayed to hear a whine in his voice.

Pat looked at him sadly.

"I knows you're a good man Frank. I mean to right the wrong we done in this valley, and I'm a-going down that tunnel now. I'll leave it between you and your God whether you come or not."

With that Pat turned and walked down towards the entrance to the tunnel.

Frank sighed and stood.

I wouldn't be alive without him. From now on, where he goes, I go. That's what he'd told Jake. That's what he'd promised himself.

And that's what I'm going to do. I can't let any more good men die because I stood aside and did nothing.

He caught up with the big man, lit two of the oil lamps, and together they went down into the tunnel.

Chapter 38

The early minutes in the first stretch of tunnel were the longest of Jake's life. They stumbled, almost running, in the confined space between the scorpions, afraid to speak, afraid that at any moment one of the beasts would turn on them. They would have no time or space to use their weapons in the confined area.

The Squire's breath came fast and heavy.

"Keep up, old man," Jake whispered. The tall tail of the scorpion ahead of them twitched. Jake held his breath, but the beast kept moving forward.

The whole tunnel smelled rank; of blood, gore and the high acrid odor of the scorpions themselves. The floor ran awash with slime and blood. Twice Jake's foot slid away from beneath him and he struggled to keep balance.

"Keep up, old man," the Squire whispered, and laughed.

The sound echoed around them. The scorpions, as one, stopped moving and everything went suddenly still and quiet.

The tail ahead of them swayed in the air like a snake looking for a victim to strike. The scorpion behind them inched forward slowly. In one claw it held a lump of meat the size of a human torso. That wasn't what had Jake concerned. The second claw clacked open and closed. It waved in the air, less than a foot from Jake's nose. It stopped clacking, and opened and closed slowly.

It's tasting us.

Jake and the Squire stood completely still. The only sound was their own breathing and the thudding of their heartbeats in their chests. A bead of sweat ran down Jake's nose and fell with a soft plop on the floor. The claw dived towards the noise and wafted over the ground for several seconds.

Jake held his breath.

The claw clacked twice, the noise like a gunshot in the confines of the tunnel. As if it was a signal, the line of scorpions started to move again, keeping time like a marching army.

Jake allowed himself to breathe and once more broke into the shuffling run. He looked over to the Squire and pressed a finger to his lips. The Squire got the message and they stumbled on in silence until they reached the side tunnel. The scorpions scuttled inside while the two men went straight on.

Jake turned and looked back.

The line of scorpions stretched away into the gloom, a seemingly never-ending supply of meat being delivered into the cavern below. Jake suddenly had a mental image of eggs, thousands of them, all hatching, the scorpions gorging themselves and growing as more and more meat was delivered into their claws.

He started to run.

"Come on Squire. We need to hurry."

Chapter 39

Frank and Pat arrived at the side tunnel just in time to see the last scorpion descend inside. Frank went to the lip and raised the lantern. The eggs still glistened where they hung on the walls. The young scorpions inside, now more than two inches long, writhed violently, small claws starting to tear at the thick walls that encased them.

They've grown.

They're nearly ready to hatch.

He looked down into the cave. There was no sign of any movement below, but the walls glistened. Thick layers of squirming eggs covered every surface.

If they get out, it won't just be the valley that gets overrun; it'll be the whole of Montana.

"Okay, big fella," he said. "You've convinced me. What's the plan?"

Pat lifted the axe.

"We stop any coming back out. We hold them here until Jake gets back."

And if Jake doesn't come back?

He kept that thought to himself. As Frank moved out of the cave entrance, Pat took his place and stood on guard. Frank took the time to finish the pipe, smoking it down to the very last embers until they finally winked out.

There was a scuttling in the side passage and a clack. They saw the claw first, rising above floor level. Pat hacked, just once, with the axe. Yellow fluid sprayed as the claw span away into darkness. A conical snout came up. Pat kicked out. The beast fell away. The loud clacking of claws echoed up from below, but nothing else came up the tunnel.

One at a time we can handle. But what if they come in a group?

Come on Jake.

We need that powder.

Chapter 40

Ruby Creek felt quiet and strangely normal as Jake and the Squire emerged from the mine and squinted against the sudden daylight.

"I've thought of a flaw in the plan, Gaffer," the Squire said. "How in the name of the Lord are we going to carry the powder back up that slope.

Jake smiled grimly.

"We've just got to carry what we can. We ain't got no horses...and they wouldn't go up into the tunnel anyway."

The Squire was quiet as they walked down to the storage cabin, and both of them avoided looking too closely at where Strang's body still lay outside the other cabin. Coyotes had been at him. The body sat in a pool of guts and gore.

The Squire helped Jake bring the powder kegs out onto the porch. There were six of them, small barrels each about a foot long and the same wide.

"Ain't gonna be able to carry more than two each," Jake said.

The Squire held up an empty burlap grain-sack.

"You'll get three in here, I reckon," he said.

Jake nodded.

"Good find. Now all we need is another like that."

They went back into the storeroom. Jake found what he was looking for seconds later. He placed a spool of fuse wire in his jacket pocket.

Looks to be a couple of yards of it. That should be plenty.

It was only then that he noticed the Squire had stopped searching.

The Englishman spoke softly.

"I've been thinking, Gaffer," he said. "You've got a bag of gold squirreled away here somewhere. Why don't we just take it and high-tail it out of here?"

I done had the same thought myself... many times.

"I made promises, Squire," Jake replied. "Hard promises. If I done broke them, I wouldn't be any kind of man at all."

The Squire nodded.

"I thought you would say that. But you see," he said, taking out his pistol. "I made no such promises."

He pointed the gun at Jake.

"So why don't you be a good fellow and tell me where the gold is. I'll be on my way, and you can go and be a good hero. That way, everyone will be happy."

Jake stared down the barrel.

"We ain't got time for shenanigans, Squire. This powder is needed up in the cave. You know that."

The Squire smiled grimly.

"You won't be getting me back up there in a hurry. Now, where is the gold?"

"You know, Squire," Jake said. "I done had pistols pointed in my face afore. I don't scare easy."

"Don't mistake me for the lad Strang," the Englishman replied. "I'll put you down and spit on you if you try anything. We're both old enough to know what's going to happen. Just give me the gold. Time's a-wasting for your pals up in the tunnel."

I've put what we found so far in the place where Mother will never find it.

"We need to go to the main cabin," Jake said. "The gold is in the crawl-space under the floor there, under the stove. We always hid things there back at the farm. Where Mother will never find it."

"Lead on then man, lead on," the Squire said impatiently.

A cloud of blow-flies rose lazily to meet them as they entered the cabin. The room had been splattered with blood and the sickly yellow fluids of a scorpion. The stink assaulted Jake, almost like a physical blow to the face.

The Walker pistol lay on the floor. As Jake bent the Squire also noticed it.

"I reckon I'll be the one taking a look down there," he said. He motioned with the pistol.

"Just stand in the corner, Gaffer. This won't take but a minute."

Jake stepped back into the corner. The Englishman kept the pistol pointing vaguely in that direction as he pulled up two floorboards near the stove. He bent to one knee.

"There is something down here." He put his left hand down.

Clack.

The Squire's screams rang loud through the room. He pulled back his arm. Where his left hand had been was just a stump, spraying blood. The floorboards at his feet buckled and broke as a large scorpion, blood crazed, forced its way up from below.

Chapter 41

Frank's fears were realized not long after Pat kicked the scorpion down into the darkness.

It started with a rustling. The acrid odor got noticeable stronger, accompanied by more of the gunshot-fast clacking.

They're coming up the wall.

"Make your peace with the Lord," Pat said to Frank. "Here they come."

Pat raised the axe. The first scorpion to poke its snout out of the cave was immediately cleaved through the middle and kicked back down the hole. It only served to send the rest into a frenzied attack. Two more came straight behind it. Pat went for the higher one first, taking off both claws in a left-right strike.

He was going to be too slow to deal with the one that reached for his ankle. Frank fired three shots. They blew the claw into pieces of shell and gore. The recoil opened the wound at his shoulder again, and he felt blood flow inside his shirt.

That's the least of my worries.

Pat swung the axe, again and again. Frank backed him up, firing shot after shot into the seething mass of scorpions that fought and struggled to find a space to get through. The side tunnel was full of them, the noise of clacking claws louder even than Frank's gunshot.

The pistol grew hot to the touch, and still Frank reloaded and fired as fast as he was able. Pat swung the axe like a man possessed, coat fluttering around him like wings. The ground at Pat's feet ran with the sticky yellow guts of the scorpions mixed with shell and fragments of claw. The pieces cracked and split underfoot as Pat danced hither and thither to avoid slashing, clacking claws.

But even the big man couldn't hold back the press of the scorpions.

While Frank was completing yet another reload, Pat hacked a claw off an attacker, then buried the axe deep in the shell of a second. The axe caught, momentarily stuck in the shell. In the time he took to put his foot on the body and lever the axe out one of the scorpions had scuttled past him, heading straight for where Frank was still reloading.

A claw flashed, heading for his face.

Frank reversed the pistol and, using it like a club, kept the claw at bay. The thick tail swung overhead. It struck, but Frank just had time to pull his head aside. The barbed tip struck the wall by his ear. Poison splashed on rock.

The beast came on faster. One claw headed for Frank's head, the other, lower, targeting his groin.

He smacked the one nearest his head with the butt of the gun. But he had no time to get near the other.

The claw opened, wide, and Frank waited for the cut that would surely cleave him in two.

Chapter 42

Jake dived for the Walker just as the scorpion came all the way out of the floor. It grabbed the Squire round the waist with both claws. It squeezed and the Englishman collapsed inwards with a last sigh, blood pumping in gouts from his mouth.

Jake rolled and came up with the heavy pistol pointing straight at the scorpion. But it wasn't paying him any attention. It had already started to chop the Englishman up, taking him apart at waist and neck. It neatly snipped off the head which rolled and came to rest at Jake's feet, eyes staring accusingly, mouth still opening and closing as if trying to speak.

Jake kicked the head away.

The scorpion had the Squire's torso in one claw and one of his legs in another. It dragged itself backward through the hole it had made in the floor.

It's going to take him up to the cave.

Jake suddenly got an idea.

Probably the worst one I ever had, but Mama Stratford always told me I ain't had no smarts since they first skelped my ass.

He ran from the cabin to the storeroom and stuffed three barrels of powder into the burlap sack. He had to drop the Walker to do it, and looked ruefully at the pistol.

Just when I need you most, I ain't gonna be able to take you.

He dragged the sack behind him back to the main cabin. The scorpion had just emerged from the crawlspace, carrying the bloody parts of the squire aloft. Jake drew his saber and leapt onto its back. He almost lost his balance but was able to stick the saber through one of the shell ridges and hold on. The tall tail swayed less than a foot from Jake's head, but it was as if the beast did not even realize he was there. He dragged the sack up beside him and held on.

The scorpion carried him up towards the mine.

Chapter 43

The claw came down towards Frank's groin. It opened… and closed on a small stone spear that came from Frank's left side. Another spear flew and bored a hole in the top of the shell.

Frank rolled away. More pain flared at his shoulder.

The cave uphill from them was filled with the small people. They looked at Pat with something that looked like reverence.

It's the clothes.

They think the Pastor has come back from the dead.

And maybe he has.

Pat hacked from left to right with the axe, too busy to look around. A large barbed tail swung over his head, getting ready to strike. Two of the small people leapt onto it, holding tight as it swung, not letting go even as it dashed their bodies against the rock. More of the little people ran forward to Pat's side. They thrust spears at anything that moved in the tunnel.

Their actions gave Pat some breathing room. He took the tail off a scorpion with one mighty slice, then split another down the middle. When he kicked that one down into the tunnel the remainder of the scorpions scuttled away, down into the darkness.

Frank leant back against the tunnel wall and sucked air until he felt he could move without puking.

Pat stayed at the side-tunnel entrance, legs splayed, axe raised. The little people crowded around him, stroking the duster and the cassock underneath.

Well, the Pastor wanted to bring religion to the heathen.

It sure looks like he's managed it.

Frank loaded the pistol with the last of his cartridges.

Far down in the depths of the cave the clacking started up again.

They're coming back.

Come on Jake.

Where in Hell are you?

Chapter 44

Jake was in his own personal hell. They had long since left daylight behind. Now he bounced, with an unsure grip, on the back of the giant scorpion. They sped along a pitch-black tunnel. Somewhere, not far enough away, a barbed tail hung, ready to strike at the merest provocation.

It felt like they had been in darkness for hours. Jake's arm felt stiff and sore, cramping badly where it gripped tight at the burlap sack. He had the other arm locked stiff, gripping with all his strength at the hilt of the saber.

The scorpion moved with a scuttling, rolling gait that shook pieces of the Squire's innards free with each jolt. A long rope of slimy gut fell across Jake's face and slid away. Blood spattered, and no matter how much Jake tried, some of it got in his mouth causing him to gag and choke.

I ain't so sure those promises are worth it George.

Finally, after what felt like an eternity, he saw light in the distance ahead.

Just as he started to celebrate, he saw a muzzle flash and a second later a shot rang out. The ball hit the scorpion less than six inches from Jake's hand. Pieces of shell and gore splashed over his hand and the smell got much worse.

"It's me, Jake," he shouted. "Let it through."

Jake let go of the saber and rolled away. The scorpion stopped, momentarily confused, then moved forward again.

As Jake looked up he saw Frank move to one side to let the beast pass. Behind Frank, Pat did the same.

And so did a large group of the little people.

Just like Pat.

Leave him alone for a minute and he makes a crowd of new friends.

The beast went down the tunnel with the remaining pieces of the

Squire. A loud clacking came up from below.

Jake tried to ignore the crowd of little people who now fawned over Pat.

I'll think about that later.

He dragged the burlap sack over to the cave mouth and pulled out the fuse wire.

"Did they all go down?"

Frank shrugged. Jake saw that the man was in some pain. He sat down hard and slumped against the wall. Even in the dim light from the lamps he looked white as a sheet. His voice came as a throaty whisper.

"All the ones we saw went down into the hole. What's the plan?"

"We light the fuses, throw the powder down the hole and get the hell out of here," Jake said, smiling grimly.

For the second time, Pat contradicted Jake.

"That ain't gonna work, Jake," the big man said softly.

"Of course it'll work Pat. I got three barrels of powder here. You know how big a bang that'll make?"

Pat shook his head.

"We ain't got any way of knowing how big that cave is. There could be thousands of them things down there. We gotta close this entrance."

Jake put the barrels down.

"Pat. I've always looked after you. Trust me on this one."

Pat shook his head again.

"Ain't gonna happen, Jake. We gotta do right by these folks here, and by the folks out in our world. We gotta bring this whole tunnel down at both ends."

"Well you see Pat…" Jake began.

Frank interrupted him.

"Listen to Pat, Jake. He's right. And you know it."

I know it. Don't mean I gotta be happy about it.

Jake sighed.

"We've got a problem. We've only got about ten minutes of fuse. We won't get back down below in time."

Pat smiled a big lazy smile.

"Ain't no problem at all Jake. I'll stay here and make sure the job gets done at this end. You and Frank git down to the Creek and take care of that end. When you hear this end blow, you can blow your end, and the job's done."

"Ain't gonna happen. I ain't leaving you here Pat."

"And I ain't going back down the tunnel, so what you gonna do? Shoot me?"

The little people picked up on the aggression between the two men and crowded round Pat. Jake suddenly found himself confronted by a forest of small spears pointed aggressively in his direction.

Frank laughed.

"Looks like the big man has the upper hand, Jake."

Jake looked at Pat.

"I can't leave you big man. You're the only friend I've got left."

Pat softened.

"Somebody's gotta tell the families what happened to the rest of them. You've got to tell your family about George. You gotta git Jake. And git quick. Them beasts will be a-crawling back up here any minute now, and we'll have to hold them until you're ready at the bottom end."

"Pat. Please?" Jake felt tears come and wiped them away angrily.

"I'll be fine Jake," the big man said, looking at the little people. "All this time you looked after me. Now I'll be looking after these folks. I done remembered everything you taught me. I want to do this."

I was right.

He has changed.

He's become his own man.

Jake put out a hand and Pat shook it.

"I'll be gitting. You remember how the powder works?"

Pat replied in a perfect mimicry of Jake's own words.

"You put a length of fuse in the end, light it, and run like buggery."

He handed Pat the length of fuse and clapped him on the shoulder.

"Good luck big man. Take care of your folks."

Pat nodded.

"And you yours Jake. Now git, while the gitting's good."

Jake turned back to Frank.

"It's just you and me then, Greyback."

Frank coughed, but didn't get up.

"I figured I'd just sit here for a while."

Frank opened his jacket. Making sure Pat's view was obscured he showed Jake a shirt seeped with blood. There was enough for it to be pooling on the ground around his thighs.

"I made a promise too," Frank said. "To look after the big man. I figure I'll stay and make sure he keeps out of trouble."

He put out a hand.

"Been a pleasure Jake."

Jake shook the offered hand.

"You're a good man Frank Collins."

Frank coughed, and blood came up.

"I'm working on it."

Jake rose. He had one last look at Pat. The little people were crowded around him, three deep.

"You sure about this, Pat?"

"More sure than I've ever been. Git going, Jake, before I start crying."

The old Pat would've been crying long ago.

Jake lifted one of the oil lamps, turned, and ran down the tunnel.

Chapter 45

"You okay, Frank?" Pat asked after the light from Jake's lamp faded down into the distance.

Frank nodded. He was glad of the extra darkness. Pat wouldn't be able to see the amount of blood he'd lost.

"Bring those barrels over to me big fella. I'll get the fuses in and ready."

Pat dropped the sack at Frank's feet, handed him the length of fuse, and went back to stand guard at the cave-mouth. Frank reached for the sack. Something else inside him tore. Pain flared through the left side of his body.

Ain't going nowhere anytime soon Frank. Best get used to the idea.

He felt weak and dizzy. His vision came and went, darkness growing at the corners. But he had enough strength left to get three fuses into the barrels.

"How long you want them set for Pat?"

"Three minutes at most," Pat said. "That's enough time for us to run back up top I reckon."

Run? I can't hardly stand.

He set the fuses short, no more than thirty seconds, and laid the barrels down beside him.

Jake had only been gone five minutes. They needed to give him at least twenty to get down to the Creek and back to the shaft with some powder.

If we are given the time.

Down in the pit the clacking came louder, and along it, the now familiar rustling.

Here they come.

The small people threw a volley of spears down the shaft. The scurrying got louder. A wave of scorpions tried to force their way out of the pit.

Pat and the small people joined them in battle.

141

Chapter 46

Jake ran down through the cave as fast as he dared. Several times he tripped, almost fell, but somehow managed to keep his balance. His mind was full of images, of Pat being torn apart by giant claws, of Frank foaming at the mouth as a poison barb was pulled from his chest.

No. I won't be letting that happen anytime soon.

He burst out into daylight like all the hounds of hell were at his ass and slid down the hill to the storeroom.

Two minutes later he was on his way back up to the shaft, a barrel of powder under each arm and the loaded Walker pistol shoved inside his belt.

Chapter 47

Pat swung the axe with a ferocity Frank had never seen before.

He has become a force of nature himself. Every bit a creature of the valley, as much as the big cat, or the wolves.

Bizarrely the small people started to sing, a chant that Frank nearly recognized.

And so I should. It is the song the Pastor sang at the end.

The small people didn't form any words, but Pat picked up on the tune and soon the cave resounded and echoed with his booming song.

Then let our songs abound, and every tear be dry,

We're marching through Immanuel's ground, to fairer worlds on high.

We're marching to Zion, beautiful, beautiful Zion.

We're marching upward to Zion, the beautiful city of God.

Tens of the Scorpions fell beneath the axe. But more came on, filling the cave-mouth.

Something fell to the floor at Pat's feet and scurried into the darkness. But not before Frank saw what it was.

The first of the young have hatched.

The small ones had seen it. They stamped their feet in time with their chanting, killing the hatchlings that had fallen.

Then they surprised Frank. Ten of them left Pat's side. At first he thought they were going to flee. But they had other ideas.

The small people leapt headlong into the cavern, stabbing at the scorpions even as the clacking claws dismembered them.

The press of the scorpions grew less and once more they retreated to the depths. Pat was left with twenty of more of the small people, standing in a pool of gore, broken shell, claws and dismembered limbs.

"Time you were going, Pat," Frank said softly. Blood bubbled at his lips.

Pat was at his side in seconds. Frank saw, not entirely surprised, that

Pat's beard was going to grow in gray.

"Set the fuses, Frank," Pat said. "Let's get you outta here."

Frank managed to smile.

"It's my turn to help you big man."

He showed Pat the extent of his bleeding.

"I'm a goner. Take your people and get out of here."

The old Pat would have wept and pleaded.

Not this one.

Pat nodded.

"How long do we have?"

"Let's just say, I think you should run."

Pat looked around at the small people. They still fawned over him. They looked like they would fight to the death to save him.

"I'm gonna bring the Lord's word to these heathen," Pat said. "I'm gonna give them some old time religion."

I think you already have big fella.

Frank coughed and blood came up.

"Best get going big man. I don't have long left here, and you don't want to be anywhere near when I light the fuse. You'll be in the dark for a bit. I'm gonna need the lamp."

Pat nodded.

"Jake was right. You're a good man, Frank Collins. I'll be praying for you."

A second later he was gone into the darkness, the small people padding along silently beside him.

Silence fell.

Well this is a good plan, Frank Collins.

Strangely he felt at peace.

I found the solitude I was looking for.

The clacking resumed in the cavern below. Frank removed one of the side panels from the lamp, exposing the flame. Even that act brought lancing pain in his side. He pulled the barrel and the lamp close as the scuttling noise came from below.

Chapter 48

Jake was breathing heavily by the time he arrived at the shaft. He placed the barrels on the ground at the entrance and bent double, sucking up air. He had just about relaxed when he heard rocks fall somewhere close by. He got the Walker out just as a huge scorpion clambered up the hill towards him. It carried what looked like half of a horse above its head.

Jake was standing directly between it and the shaft.

He rolled to one side just as the tail swung towards him, but the beast looked more intent on taking the food back up the slope. Another scorpion followed the first, this one carrying the other half of the horse.

Jake saw an immediate problem. Neither beast was going to make it through the narrow shaft carrying such a large slab of meat. They blocked the entrance.

And I can't get at the fuses.

Chapter 49

The scorpions came up out of the cavern in a rush. And it wasn't just the large ones. The cave floor was quickly covered with the newly hatched young, a swarm of them, homing in on Frank like ants to a honey-pot.

Frank waited till the last possible second. A large scorpion closed its claw around his torso.

At the last, it wasn't Pat or Jake that came to his mind. It was the boys he'd left on the field of Shiloh.

Break out the rum lads, I'm coming home.

Frank lit the fuse.

Chapter 50

Jake moved as soon as he heard the rumble from above. He rolled twenty yards down the slope, turned and fired.

The pistol kicked like a mule. It threw Jake backward down the rest of the hill so he didn't see the immediate results.

But his shot had hit the powder.

The concussion of the explosion deafened him and set his head ringing. When he stood up it was just in time to see the mine collapse in on itself. A giant claw waved feebly in the air before being crushed under the rock fall. The explosion set off a landslide high above and Jake had to retreat fast as mud, earth and rock fell in a long slide, covering the shaft in tons of rubble.

Chapter 51

Jake walked out of Ruby Creek ten minutes later. He carried a pair of saddlebags; one side heavy with food, the other with the small bag he's found where Mother would never find it.

Far out in the lake something large splashed.

Jake gave the water a wide berth and set his gaze on the long trek out of the valley.

About the Author

William Meikle is a Scottish genre writer who has been called the "Master of Pulp Fiction." He has had more than 130 short stories and 10 novels published and has graced the Number One spot on Amazon's bestseller list several times.

Made in the USA
Coppell, TX
16 September 2022

83222160R00090